WITCH WAY DOWN UNDER

THE WITCH WAY MYSTERIES - BOOK 3

JANE HINCHEY

BAYWOLF PRESS

BP

BAYWOLF PRESS

For Petrina,
thank you for letting me use your name.

AUTHOR'S NOTE

Hey there! Welcome to a whirlwind of whimsy and wonder in my Witch Way Mysteries. If you've got a soft spot for the supernatural, you're in for a real treat.

This is your gateway to a world where magic and mystery intertwine. The Witch Way series has now woven its full tale, but the magic doesn't stop here. For news on my latest adventures and stories, don't forget to sign up for my newsletter.

Janehinchey.com/subscribe

Are you ready to conjure up some fun and unravel a few bewitching puzzles? I'll see you on the other side!

xoxo
Jane

ABOUT THIS BOOK

Tick Tock. Time is running out.

My parents are missing in outback Australia. Only they've left me clues. Clues that tell me they were close to a significant discovery—the location of a copper scroll that leads to untold treasures. A scroll that treasure hunters would kill for.

Now I'm in a race against time. Together with my Gran, best friend Jenna, my familiar Archie, and bad boy lawyer Blake Tennant, we head to an outback town called Arrowstrand, where the locals are hiding their own secrets, and I must rely on my magic and blind faith to venture into the unknown.

The stakes have never been higher; can I reach my parents before it's too late or will they be lost forever?

"Oh, good grief." Jenna pinched her nose and waved her hand in front of her face. "Who farted? Archie? Was that you?"

Archie lifted his orange head, twitched an ear, and eyeballed Jenna with such a look of disdain that I couldn't contain a snort of amusement. "More likely it was Gran," I said.

We both looked at Gran, who was dozing in her seat, head lolling against the travel pillow around her neck. We were in a private jet, headed to Australia. I was still in a state of shock. Not only because my parents were missing, but also that Blake had procured the use of a private jet to transport not only me, but my cat, my Gran, and one of my best friends to the other side of the world to search for them. Blake was still a mystery to me. A very distracting, very hot mystery. He was Gran's lawyer. My dad had called him when she'd been arrested for Bonnie Emerson's murder. Yet despite the endless questions I'd thrown at him, he'd yet to reveal exactly how he knew my dad.

Jenna, being a journalist for the *Whitefall Cove Tribune*, always had a nose for a story and she'd immediately dug into the man who was Blake Tennant. He was a partner at the law firm, Richards, Jones and Tennant, and Jenna had yet to uncover who the Jones was in that partnership. Speculation was rife it was my father—although he was a professor and an archaeologist, not a lawyer. Blake had remained tight-lipped each time we'd brought it up, which was a lot. He'd simply say Dad was a friend and change the subject.

"What has she been eating?" Jenna grumbled, still waving her hand to dispel the smell.

"I don't know," I replied. "Could be anything really." Even as I spoke a little *prft* of sound came from Gran and I bit back another laugh. "Brace yourself," I said to Jenna. "Incoming."

"Oh my God!" Jenna wailed, loud enough that Gran stirred, cracked open an eye, then slipped back into slumber.

Archie, who'd been curled up on the seat next to

me lifted his head and sniffed the air, then promptly jumped down and headed toward the back of the jet. We'd set up a tray for him in the bathroom, along with a bowl of water and some dry food. I watched until he disappeared into the bathroom, his tail twitching.

It was surreal we were on our way to Australia. I shuddered to think how much this little expedition was costing—and I sincerely hoped I would not be presented with a bill at the end. I'd asked Blake, and he'd told me not to worry about it, that it was taken care of. Still, I couldn't help but feel a little uneasy about the whole situation. I didn't like to think of myself as a charity case; I liked to pay my own way, but getting Archie on a commercial flight all the way to Australia just would not happen. Somehow Blake had circumnavigated quarantine requirements and Archie had a special dispensation to enter any country I cared to take him to. That told me that Blake was a powerful man. Or he had powerful connections, because really, who could do that?

The chirping of my laptop interrupted my train of thought. Monica was face timing me. Hitting connect, I smiled at the dark-haired beauty on my screen.

"How's it going, Mon?"

"All good this end. Wendy is doing just fine at the bookstore. Bruce is helping too."

"Excellent, thank you." The Dusty Attic was the

bookstore I'd recently purchased in Whitefall Cove. I'd considered closing it while I was away, but Wendy had convinced me to let her run it in my absence. Despite being heavily pregnant, she'd been positive she could manage, provided I was okay with her soon-to-be husband Bruce helping.

"You nearly there?" Monica asked.

I nodded. "I think we've only got a couple of hours to go. It's been a long trip. We've only had to refuel once, but I gotta say, flying in a private jet is the way to go, it's so darn comfortable."

Monica frowned. "Don't tell me. I don't want to hear it." She grumbled, "If it weren't for the fact that the Australian sun would surely fry me in two seconds flat, I'd be there with you."

"I know you would. But you're still helping. Keeping an eye on the store for me. I appreciate it." Monica was a vampire, and while she could tolerate short bursts of sunlight, extended periods would burn her to a crisp. And where we were going, the Australian outback, just would not work for her. Not this time anyway.

After chatting with Monica for a few more minutes, I hung up just as Blake walked through the cabin. "Everything okay?" he asked, pausing by my seat. He looked as delicious as always, snug jeans hugging his thighs, dark T-shirt clinging to rock-hard abs. He carried that bad boy vibe with him, and as much as it attracted me, I was cautious at the same time. After the kiss we'd shared on my doorstep before he'd dropped the bombshell of my parents' disappearance, we hadn't had a chance to be alone—or talk about what that kiss had meant. If anything.

"Sure." I shrugged. "Why wouldn't it be?"

He opened his mouth to reply only to be interrupted by Gran, who woke with a yawn, a stretch, and a loud fart. "We there yet?" she asked, unclipping her seat belt and swinging her legs from the reclining seat.

"Nearly," Blake told her. "Another hour."

"Sweet. Got time for a shower then." And off she shuffled to the bathroom that, yes, came equipped with a shower. A loud fart accompanied each step she took, as if she were gas propelled, and I giggled, more at the wide-eyed expression on Blake's face than Gran's stutter farting efforts.

"Does she always...?"

"Pretty much." I nodded.

He shook his head, a dimple showing as he smiled, then he patted my shoulder. "The pilot will let you know when to stop using electronics. Our satellite is okay until we get within Adelaide's airspace. Then we must shut it off."

That was another thing. A private jet with its own

satellite, which meant I not only had phone reception the entire way, but internet too. Despite the journey around the globe taking us almost twenty-four hours, it was in absolute comfort. Being able to sleep horizontally was a plus, with the big leather chairs reclining so we could get a decent rest.

"And then what?" I asked. "What happens when we get to Adelaide?" All I knew was that my parents had booked tickets to come home, but they'd never made their flight. The archaeological dig they were on was near a small township several hundred miles from the city of Adelaide itself.

"I've got a car waiting and we head out to Arrowstrand."

Arrowstrand was in the Flinders Ranges, about four hundred miles from the city of Adelaide. Population? Around three hundred. I'd Googled what I could about my parents' last known location, and I knew what had attracted them to the area. A fabled copper pyramid located within Grid Point 44 in the Flinders Ranges—and the whole region is a vortex zone. It had Mom and Dad's names written all over it.

Australia was not what I'd been expecting. To be honest, I don't know what I *was* expecting. Kangaroos hopping down the street, perhaps. But there were none. In fact, Adelaide looked very civilized, very... normal. Busy. Cars, buses, trains, traffic.

The heat had been a surprise. It was fall yet it was already eighty-two degrees—and it was an intense, dry heat, the sun searing. I'd exited the jet, sunglasses in place, but still I'd had to raise my arm to shield my face from the glare.

"Seriously, what do you have in here? Rocks?" Blake grumbled as he heaved my floral suitcase into the back of a gunmetal gray Land Rover that could, quite frankly, use a good wash. It was big and square and could have served time as an army vehicle. Robust was a word that came to mind. I hoped it had cushioned seats.

"Shoes," I joked, sliding my backpack off my shoulders.

Blake paused, wiping an arm across his forehead that glistened in sweat. We'd disembarked onto the tarmac and the Land Rover had been sitting waiting, a shimmer of mirage reflecting the heat.

"Holy schamoly," Gran exclaimed, fanning her face. "Sure is hot here."

"Come on." Jenna grasped her elbow and led her toward the car. "Let's jump in and get out of the sun. I hope you packed sunscreen, Gran."

Gran was nodding. "Packed my bikini too." I held open the rear door for them, chuckling when Archie streaked ahead of them and jumped onto the back seat. The rear of the Land Rover was full of our luggage plus metal boxes with padlocks.

"Whose car is this again?" I asked, moving to the front passenger side and opening the door, only to be confronted with a steering wheel.

"Right-hand drive in Australia," Blake pointed out.

"Thank you, Captain Obvious," I muttered under my breath, slamming the door and making my way to the passenger side.

"It's mine." A woman's voice startled me, and I swiveled. "Or rather, it belongs to the Bureau of Occult Research and Defense, but I drive it."

"Who are you?" I eyed her up and down. She looked like a female Indiana Jones with khaki green pants, a white tank, with a beige button-down shirt over the top, unbuttoned and tied at the waist with the sleeves rolled up. Around her neck looped a dark green cotton scarf. A canvas satchel hung off one shoulder, and a straw panama hat, with one long braid hanging over one shoulder completed the outfit. Oh, let's not forget the sturdy boots. She looked like she was ready for the Australian outback.

I, on the other hand, felt maybe I'd gotten the dress code wrong. Despite traveling with my parents as a child, it was a lifetime ago and apparently, I'd forgotten a lot. Like how to dress for an expedition. I stood in my black and white polka dot shorts, white flip-flops, a white halter top and a high ponytail. Had I even packed a hat? Or sunscreen?

"I'm Remy Leigh." She smiled and held out her hand. She indicated the black and white dog sitting patiently at her heels. "And this is Bandit."

Bandit had one ear sticking straight up, the other flopped over, but his most stunning feature was that his eyes were different colors. One brown, one a startling blue.

I shook her hand. "Harper Jones. So... this is your car? You're joining us?"

She nodded. "I'm a field agent for the Bureau. Blake asked for our help on this case."

"There you are!" Blake strode around from the rear of the car and wrapped Remy in a bear hug, squeezing her tight and making her laugh.

"How are you, big fella?" she joked. "Seb sends his regards."

"I'm good." Blake gave her the full wattage of his smile before turning it my way and I practically melted on the spot. "You two met?" he asked. I nodded, watching as Blake greeted Bandit with a ruffle of his ears.

"This is all Remy's doing." Blake waved at the Land Rover. "We're hitching a ride with her."

"Right." I guess having another person help us search for them couldn't hurt. And Remy looked like she knew what she was doing. At least she dressed the part.

"Ummm. Is Bandit going to be okay with Archie?" I glanced into the back seat where Archie sat.

"Who is Archie?" Remy asked.

"My cat."

"Oh, he'll be fine. Bandit loves cats."

"Not to eat I hope," I muttered under my breath, but Remy heard me and laid a hand on my arm.

"Seriously, he won't hurt your cat. In fact, he'll probably become best friends with him. Bandit has a habit of becoming best friends with every creature he meets."

Before I could stop her, she opened the back door and emitted a shrill whistle. Bandit leaped inside, sniffed at Archie, then lay down on the floor. Remy walked around to the driver's side and climbed in. Blake took the passenger seat, leaving me the back seat with our respective pets, and Gran and Jenna.

"So far I'm loving Australia!" Gran grinned, patting my knee. I grinned. So far all we'd seen was the airport!

"Which way are you going?" Blake asked Remy as she gunned the engine. "Highway One to Port Augusta and then up?"

She shook her head. "We'll take the B80 most of the way, then it'll be dirt roads to Arrowstrand." She turned to look at me over her shoulder. "We'll go past

Chambers Gorge and Sacred Canyon, both sites of significance and places your parents stayed before moving on to Arrowstrand."

Sites of significance. Those were the types of words Mom and Dad used to throw around.

"Do you know what my parents were working on?" I asked after Remy had pulled out into the flow of traffic leaving the airport. "All I could work out from Google was that the area they were staying is famous for a mythical copper pyramid."

"Have you heard of the treasure of the Copper Scroll?" she asked, moving into the left lane before stopping at the lights. I was glad she was driving; everything was backward in Australia. Not only was she on the wrong side of the vehicle, but the cars were traveling on the wrong side of the road!

"It's a scroll, made of copper, with a list of locations where treasure—gold and silver—had been hidden," Blake answered for me. "Discovered in 1952, although the scroll itself is said to have dated back to 30 BCE."

"You've done your homework." Remy cut him a glance before turning her attention back to the road. "Rumor has it there is another scroll. An actual map. With far more—or maybe just undiscovered—treasures," she said.

"And my parents are searching for it? In Australia? Is that where the first scroll was found?" I asked.

"No, they found the first scroll in some caves near a town called Kalya in Israel."

"Wait, now I'm really confused." I scratched my head. "So you're telling me one scroll, made of copper, was found in Israel and my parents think there is a second copper scroll in Australia? That makes no sense."

"You were right when you mentioned that within the Flinders Ranges there is supposedly a Copper Pyramid, and that within that Pyramid the remaining copper scroll is hidden. Grid points are the connection between dimensions and your father had a theory—that Grid Point 44 created an artificial time warp where travelers from ancient civilizations used it to travel to a far-off secret land."

"Australia?" I said incredulously.

"Exactly." She nodded. "It makes perfect sense. Australia was so remote, unreachable by any other means. So, if you wanted to hide something..."

"You'd get yourself to a grid point and use it like a wormhole," Blake cut in.

"Yes, but a copper pyramid isn't something you could easily hide," I pointed out. "I mean that sucker would be visible for miles."

"And yet it hasn't been discovered," Remy said.

"Maybe that's because it's a story that someone made up?"

"Could be." Remy agreed, expertly maneuvering us

through the traffic as she spoke. "But your dad shared his theory with me, and I figured if he was going to invest time and money into searching for it, then there has to be some merit behind it. Your dad is a smart man. Wives' tales wouldn't fool him."

"How do you know him?" I asked.

She adjusted the rear-view mirror and met my eyes. "He used to be my professor, back in the day. He's the one that got me interested in archeology, artifacts, and the paranormal."

"Right. And you kept in touch?"

She shrugged. "Sure. I've met your dad and mom several times when they came into Adelaide from time to time. We'd have lunch or dinner; they'd share what they were up to with their dig."

"For a mythical pyramid made from copper. Wait a minute—you don't think they could have been sucked through this worm hole, do you?" I leaned forward and grabbed the back of Blake's seat.

Remy and Blake exchanged a look. My head swiveled between them.

"You do think that!" I exclaimed, my heart thundering in my chest and my panic level rising. "So, they could have been dragged into the past?"

"Harper," Blake said, tone soothing, "take a breath."

"All we know is that your parents are not responding. We've lost communication with them,"

Remy said soothingly. "They may not be missing at all."

I flopped back against my seat. She had a point. We knew nothing for sure. They missed a flight. A flight they'd booked in a hurry. Maybe they hadn't allowed themselves enough time to get back to Adelaide? Maybe they had broken down? Or maybe they'd changed their minds? Figured Blake was on hand to take care of Gran's murder charge and had stayed put.

But they'd have told me if that were the case.

"Maybe their phone is damaged?" I said out loud.

"It's possible," Remy agreed. "Arrowstrand is remote, with limited resources. There is cell reception, but if a phone tower is out, then yeah, no phone coverage."

"You've contacted the authorities?" Blake asked Remy.

She nodded. "Affirmative. We have lodged a missing person's report—but they must speak with you, Harper, to confirm."

"Why?"

"Because you're next of kin. You spoke to them last; you knew their movements—or proposed movements. They have accepted my report and are keeping an eye out for your parents' vehicle, see if it turns up anywhere. We'll call in when we arrive and get an update. And we need to find out if foul play was involved."

A shiver ran up my spine. There were people out there who would kill for a copper scroll that led to untold riches.

CHAPTER

TWO

The rugged, weathered peaks and rocky gorges of the Flinders Ranges created a dramatic and beautiful backdrop and I sat with my eyes glued to the window, taking in the stunning countryside.

Remy played tour guide. "Wilpena Pound, from the air, looks like a massive bowl—or a crater—and spans sixty-two miles wide, but the rim is actually made up of the stumps of huge mountains, believed to be as high as the Himalayas, that have eroded over thousands of years."

"It is gorgeous," I said as we approached, the late afternoon sun casting a red shadow over the rocks in front of us as we wound our way toward them. Jenna and Gran were as enthralled as I was.

"You should see it from the air." Remy grinned.

"It's pretty amazing. If we have time, maybe Blake will take you up."

"Maybe," he said, leaning forward and peering out the windscreen at the vista before us.

We'd been in the car for five hours and I was overjoyed at the prospect of finally reaching our destination. Sitting back, I lapsed into silence, watched the breathtaking scenery of trees and rock formations as we made our way through the gorge. Despite the big green trees, the earth was dry and red and the sign that read Ikara Flinders Ranges National Park told me we were 430 miles north of Adelaide. It may as well have been a million miles for it felt like we were in another world altogether.

Remy pointed out the window. "What you see around you? Eight hundred million years old! Mind blowing, huh? And this region has been home to the Adnyamathanha people for tens of thousands of years."

"Adnyamathanha?" I butchered the word, cringing, but she didn't take offence.

"The traditional owners of this land. And it's rumored the whole area of the Flinders is a vortex zone."

I believed it, all right. I could feel the power humming in the air, my body tingling with it.

It was another two hours on the road, leaving the paved roads on the final leg of our journey and bouncing over rocky, barely there dirt tracks through rolling hills and red rocky escarpments before we finally arrived at Arrowstrand.

Remy slowed the Land Rover as we made our way down the main street, what there was of it. To the left a small church, stone cottages, a general store, bakery and café, then a hotel. To the right a post office, more cottages, a house with a police sign hanging out front, and an old stone building with an archway that read "Memorial Hall."

"This place used to be a mining town," Remy said, indicating to turn right just before the gas station on the corner. "Back when there was copper in the ground."

"Mined out?" Blake said, pushing his sunglasses to the top of his head as he surveyed the town.

"You got it." Remy nodded. "Mines are still here, just not operational. The Caravan Park is a few miles down here. You'll be surprised."

"Caravan park?" I asked.

"Trailer park," Remy explained. "Your parents' trailer is there. This was their base, and they traveled out to the Arrowstrand Caves every day."

I remembered the photos Mom had sent of the trailer they'd bought when they'd first arrived in Australia almost a year and a half ago. They'd intended to travel around Australia and visit not only sites of archeological interest but tourist destinations as well.

"How do you know that?" Gran piped up. She'd been quiet throughout the trip and I'd been worried she was car sick and likely to puke all over us. Thankfully, that hadn't turned out to be the case.

"I called the park and asked." Remy shrugged. "When Blake called Seb to ask for our help, the first thing I did was find where they were based."

"Seb is the Director of the Bureau of Occult Research and Defense," Blake explained, turning to look at us over his shoulder. "It's their jet we borrowed to get here."

Well, that was a shock. I'd thought it was Blake's jet, or at least his law firm's. To find out it belonged to the Bureau that I'd never heard of before was surprising. I mean, why would they send a jet to pick us up? It would have had to cost an absolute fortune. The longer I spent with Blake the less I knew about him. After the kiss he'd planted on me back home I'd been expecting... more. Instead, he'd stonewalled me. Every question went unanswered. He'd deftly steer the conversation back to me and it was niggling at me how little I knew about him. And watching him with Remy, clearly she knew him well. They'd greeted each other affectionately, and yet he hadn't mentioned her at all.

We drove for another ten minutes, turned down a narrow dirt track, winding around rock formations, through dried-out creek beds, over hills that resembled small mountains, but it was well worth the effort, for it was stunning.

Gum trees as far as the eye could see, leaves of green and trunks of white, and then suddenly you're in a massive clearing, at the far end a cliff with a waterfall cascading down into a waterhole. In the middle of it all a big white house with a wraparound deck. One end had been closed in and a painted sign above the door said "Office."

I spotted cabins dotted throughout the park, paths with rocks as borders, a large barbecue area sheltered beneath a wooden structure. Big trees dotted around the park, but despite the greenery the earth was dry, red, and dusty.

Someone had outlined a parking area with logs in the dirt and Remy pulled up in a cloud of dust.

"This is beautiful, absolutely stunning." I breathed, opening the door, only to have Bandit launch over the top of me, eager to explore. Archie followed.

"Here, boy." Remy snapped her fingers, and he immediately returned to her side, but his whole body was quivering with excitement.

"It sure is," Blake agreed, climbing out and tilting his head back to look at the sheer wonder of the waterfall. Gran and Jenna joined us, looking around at the huge trees towering overhead, necks craned. Then our attention was drawn to the waterfall, an oasis in the dry, desert like earth.

Gran linked her arm with mine and leaned close to murmur in my ear, "You got any sense of her?" I knew she was referring to Mom without having to ask. Gran had been uncharacteristically silent because she was worried about her only daughter. And who could blame her?

"Not yet," I whispered, "but I will try to astral walk tonight. I'm hoping now I'm closer I'll be able to connect." I'd tried in Whitefall Cove and kept coming up blank. I'd been unable to contact Mom or Dad. We'd discussed it with our coven and had surmised that possibly the physical distance between us had been too great and that I should attempt it again once we'd reached their camp.

"I'll go check us in," Blake said, heading up the stairs to the deck.

"I'm coming with you." I turned to Jenna who was standing behind me. "Could you keep an eye on this lot, make sure no-one wanders off?" My eyes moved from Gran to Archie and back again. They were both as bad as each other, you had to have eyes in the back of your head to keep track.

"Sure." Jenna smiled and slid her arm through Gran's left arm while I disentangled myself from her right.

"I think that's Mom and Dad's trailer over there." I

pointed to a big white trailer parked near the rocks. "It looks like the photos they sent me. Did you want to stay in the trailer? Or a cabin?"

"Cabin, please." Gran was frowning. "Never liked trailers. They move about too much."

"Okay, let me go organize our accommodation and then we'll get unpacked and see about dinner, okay?"

Gran nodded, and I frowned, worried again about how subdued she was, but then I had to remember that she was eighty years old and I dragged her to the other side of the world. Not that she'd have agreed to stay home, she'd made that abundantly clear.

As if reading my mind, she reached out and seized my hand. "I just need a nap, then food, and I'll be right as rain," she told me. "I'm looking forward to getting to know some of these Aussie men." She winked, and I finally felt myself relax. That was more like the Gran I knew and loved.

I followed Blake and Remy into the small office. A bell chimed when we opened the door, alerting the residents of the house they had a customer. A woman in her early forties appeared from the doorway that joined the office to the rest of the house. Dressed in cutoff denim shorts, a faded Doctor Who T-shirt, bare feet and her hair cropped close to her scalp in an orange shade that could only have come out of a box, she looked us up and down.

"Good afternoon." She smiled, showing slightly

yellow, crooked teeth. "Welcome to Arrowstrand Caravan Park."

"Afternoon." Remy took the lead, stepping forward and resting her hands on the counter. "I'm Remy Leigh. We spoke on the phone?"

"Ah yes, you're here about the Joneses, right?" Her eyes moved from Remy to Blake, then me.

"That's right. This is Blake Tennant and Harper Jones."

"You must be the daughter." She nodded. "Sorry, where are my manners! I'm Andi Webb. My family owns the land where the Arrowstrand Caves are located. It's been in Colin's—that's my husband— family for generations. Used to be a working sheep station till they went under. Sold off a heap of land but kept the caves and surrounding land, figured we'd turn it into a tourist destination."

"About my parents..." I prompted. I'd been patient for the last twenty-four hours, but now we were so close, I could feel anticipation crawling across my skin like a thousand ants. I needed to find them, now.

"Of course. Here's what I know, which isn't much. Tamir said he heard their four-wheel drive leave around ten o'clock Thursday night. They haven't returned." She looked at me, her eyes apologetic. "After Remy called me, I tried their satellite phone and couldn't get an answer. I also tried their radio but got no response."

"You weren't worried they didn't come back?" Blake asked.

She was shaking her head. "They often camped out at the caves. We're used to their comings and goings. I'm sure there's nothing to be alarmed about. Maybe they've gone deeper into the caves as they explore further. Neither satellite phone nor radio work in the caves."

"Did they take enough supplies to be gone this long?" It had been five days since they'd last been seen.

"I can't say. But they are experienced campers. They wouldn't have taken unnecessary risks or gone anywhere unprepared. Although it is unusual for them to leave the caravan park that late at night."

"They'd booked flights back to Whitefall Cove. Family emergency," Remy said.

Andi frowned. "So if they flew back to America, why are you all here?"

"Because they never made that flight," Blake said. "This is the last place someone saw them."

"Oh!" Andi flattened a palm against her chest. "I didn't know. Do the police know?"

Remy was already nodding. "I've informed them. We'll see Officer…" Remy paused, trying to recall the name of the police officer she'd been dealing with.

"That would be Sergeant Mick Gould," Andi supplied with a smile. "He's Officer in Charge around these parts, oversees the SES and CFS." At our confused faces she elaborated, "State Emergency Service and Country Fire Service. A town our size doesn't have paid employees for these things, so we rely on volunteers and Mick keeps them all in order. Well, as best he can." She rubbed her hands together. "So you're staying for a bit?"

"Yes, a few days, possibly longer," Remy said. "We'll need five cabins."

"Oh, if you have a spare key to Mom and Dad's trailer, I'll stay in that," I jumped in. "So only four cabins."

"Let me look." Andi heaved a large book onto the counter and opened it, running her finger down the page. "We have a group coming in a few days, but that still leaves enough cabins to spare, so we're good. Tamir and Omar have one each, and Nigel—he's our guide—has one of the on-site vans."

"If you don't have room, I've got camping gear and can set myself up in a tent if need be," Remy offered.

"Nah, it's fine." Andi looked at me. "I have a key to your parents' van. They're paying extra for me to change the linens and towels." She pulled out a metal box, unlocked it and rummaged around, pulling out a key with a red tag and holding it up. "Here you go, love. All yours. No charge for you since your parents are already paying site hire."

"Thank you." I took the key from her and turned it over and over, hoping to get something from it, anything, but all I got was the feel of plastic and metal, no magic residue.

Blake and Remy completed the rest of the bookings, Remy sliding a black credit card across the counter while Andi handed over keys and a hand-held CB radio.

"You'll have to share," she said. "We're on channel 15, we use CTCSS so you won't get other chatter."

"CTCSS?" Blake asked.

"Continuous tone coded squelch system." Andi grinned, seemingly proud that she knew the answer. "Basically it means that a group of radios set with the same tone can use a channel without hearing other radios using that channel. We don't have an infinite supply of channels. Stay off channel Nineteen, the truckies get cranky if you chitchat there. And five is the emergency channel—for road weather warnings, bush fires, that type of thing."

"And you said you couldn't get hold of my parents on their radio?"

"That's right. But that's not surprising if they're in the caves. The radio doesn't work in there."

"You mentioned Tamir and Omar," Blake said, picking up the radio and pocketing his key. "Who are they?"

"Oh, they're tourists. Been here over a week. Hired Nigel for a couple of days to take them to the caves and show them around. They're probably there now. My husband, Colin, runs a four-wheel-drive tour business. He's out most days, takes a lot of folks out from town who don't want to necessarily stay this far out. We recycle our water, our power is sporadic—although we have backup generators so don't be alarmed. We run mostly on solar. Mobile phone service drops in and out, which is why we also have a satellite phone, and the radios."

We thanked Andi and were leaving when Andi came hurrying after me, linens and towels in her arms. "I haven't changed the linens yet. I was due to do them tomorrow, but I can do them now."

"That's okay, just give them to me. I'll do it."

"Are you sure?" Andi looked surprised, as if she'd never had a guest offer to make their own beds before.

"Seriously, I don't mind." I smiled reassuringly and took the linens from her.

"Well... okay. Thank you." She ran a hand across her cropped hair. "Yell out if you need anything. You must book Nigel if you want him to take you to the caves."

"We'll let you know," Blake said with a smile, before holding open the door and letting me and Remy proceed outside in front of him.

At the bottom of the stairs Remy turned. "I'll bring the Land Rover over so we can unpack your gear first. Archie is probably dying for a drink and something to eat." As if he sensed we were talking about him, Archie trotted across to us, meowing and rubbing around my ankles. With my arms full I couldn't pick him up and was considering how I could juggle the linens and Archie when Blake interceded.

"Here, boy." He scooped Archie up in his arm and I blinked at him in surprise. "Go unlock the trailer. I'm right behind you." He nudged me forward.

Right. Squaring my shoulders, I walked across the hard-packed dirt to where the trailer was parked, about a hundred meters from the house. No paved pathways out here. As I approached, I could see they had hidden power lines in the trees sprouting from the rock wall, running along behind the trailer and on to the cabins further down. One other trailer was in residence. It was old and beat up and I assumed it belonged to the guide, Nigel. Judging by the weeds growing around the tires it hadn't been moved in quite a while.

With my palm suddenly sweaty, I slid the key into the lock and turned. It clicked open, and I pressed the button, opening the door and stepping up and inside. It was as if I'd been transported back in time. A childhood of camping at dig sites flooded my memory at the familiar scents. Sandalwood, leather and old cigars. But what I saw had my heart stuttering in my chest.

THREE

The trailer was a mess. Every cupboard door hung open, clothing was strewn across the bed and floor, the tabletop littered with maps and books. I frowned. This wasn't like my parents. They were neat and organized. The trunk my dad loved sat on the bed amid the chaos, open. He'd never leave it like that. I approached cautiously and peered inside. It was disorganized, as if he'd rummaged through it in a hurry. I wondered what he'd been searching for that he'd leave one of his most prize possessions like this. And out in the open. Dad usually stowed his chest in the bottom of the wardrobe, away from prying eyes.

The trailer rocked when Blake stepped inside. He closed the door behind him and set Archie down.

"Whoa!" His eyes traveled around taking in the scene. "This place looks trashed."

Thanks Captain Obvious. I bit my tongue. "Yeah."

He crossed to the table and looked down at the maps.

"They wouldn't have left the trailer like this. Mom is a neat freak," I explained, sinking down onto the end of the bed, dropping the linens by my side.

"But they left in a hurry, remember? Packed in a rush to get home to you and Gran."

"Even more reason to stow this." I thumped the side of the chest, drawing Blake's attention. "They keep important stuff in here. Like those maps? They go in here. And the notebooks and stuff. Plus, Dad's tools. He would never leave the chest out, let alone open like this."

Blake studied the trailer silently for a moment. "It looks like someone has searched the place. Pretty sure your parents wouldn't have been intending to pack crockery for the flight home." He shut the cupboard doors in the kitchen area.

I watched, still stunned to find the trailer in such a state. "All I know is that they wouldn't have left it like this."

"No signs of a struggle though. They weren't here when it happened."

The sound of the Land Rover interrupted our

musings. Remy kept the engine running while she hopped out and opened the back.

"Everything okay?" she asked when Blake and I joined her.

"Someone has been through the Jones's trailer," Blake said solemnly, lifting out my suitcase, then the box of Archie's supplies.

"Seriously?" Remy looked at me and rubbed her hand up and down my arm. "You okay, Harper?"

I smiled wanly. "I'm fine." *Liar*. Truth was I found little comfort in my parents' trailer, being amongst their belongings. I guess I'd been expecting an instant connection and when it hadn't happened... I was a little stunned. But I still had my astral walking ability, and I fully intended to put it to good use tonight. For now, I needed to sort out the mess and get Archie fed and watered.

"Let me clean this up, settle Archie and then maybe we can go find something to eat?" I suggested, glancing at my phone. Traveling across so many time zones had messed with my body clock and while the setting sun told me it was time for dinner, my body told me it was ready for breakfast.

"I gave your Gran and Jenna their keys," Remy said. "And I'm just about to drop off their luggage. Your Gran said something about a nap."

"How about we all meet up in an hour?" Blake suggested. "Enough time for us to refresh, nap, shower, whatever. Andi said the hotel in town serves a good meal."

"Should we book a table?" I asked and Remy laughed.

"No need, not in a town this size. Would you mind if I brought Bandit over to hang with Archie when we go out? He's just going to scratch at the door and howl if I leave him on his own knowing his new furry buddy is over here."

"That's fine. Drop him over when you're ready."

After they'd gone I set up Archie's litter tray, spooned his daily ration of wet food into a bowl and stroked along his back as he scarfed down his dinner, purring the entire time. "I don't know how you do that without your food going down the wrong hole."

While he ate, I tidied the trailer, made up the bed with fresh sheets, splashed water on my face in the tiny bathroom before lying on the bed and staring up at the ceiling. Archie finished eating, then jumped up by my side and busied himself grooming. The only sound was the birds outside and Archie licking. I must have dozed off because the next thing I knew Remy was banging on the door. It was time for dinner.

One other car was parked out front of the Arrowstrand Hotel when we pulled up. The rest of the main strip was deserted except for a lone dog wandering down the middle of the street. A gust of wind blew a tumbleweed past, and I immediately thought of the old western movies Gran used to watch with Pop when I was a child. Inside, however, was a different story. The place was bustling. A juke box was blaring out pop music, there was a pool table with half a dozen guys watching the two men playing, a young couple with two small children sat at a table, trying to wrangle their kids into eating the food they'd ordered rather than drop it on the table and floor.

We'd followed Gran in, who'd busted through the doors full of vigor and pep. Clearly her nap had done the trick. She'd changed outfits from the hot pink velour leisure suit she'd worn on the plane to a spaghetti strap summer dress that hit just above her sagging knees. Around her neck she'd wrapped a red and white bandanna that clashed impossibly with the purple flower print of her dress. And on her head, the pièce de résistance. A baseball cap. A grin pulled at my lips as I followed her inside. Gran had always had eclectic fashion sense—these poor Australians would have no idea what hit them.

Along the side wall was a bar, behind it, a slim woman with her back toward us, her long purple curls cascading down her back. She glanced over her shoulder when she heard the door close and gave us a big smile. It wasn't until we got closer I realized she wasn't the young woman I thought she was. She'd have to be sixty, at least, with laugh lines deeply ingrained and yet there was a youthful sparkle to her eyes. She reminded me of Gran—could have been the purple hair—and I immediately liked her.

"Welcome to Arrowstrand Hotel." She flipped a tea towel over one shoulder and turned to face us, resting her palms on the bar. "What can I get you?"

"We were told you serve meals?" Remy said, and the woman nodded.

"Sure do. Help yourself to the menus at the end there." She pointed to the far end of the bar where a sign hung down from the ceiling that read *order here.* "Then just come back here when you're ready to order. Sit anywhere."

"Thanks," we said in unison. Jenna grabbed some menus while Remy headed toward a table that would comfortably seat us all. It wasn't until I was nearly at the table that I realized Gran wasn't with us and I swiveled to find her still at the bar, chatting up a storm with the woman who'd welcomed us. I headed back to join them.

Gran introduced us. "Harper, this here is Petrina. She and her husband own this place. This is my granddaughter Harper."

Petrina leaned forward to shake my hand, her grip firm. "Pleased to meet you, Harper. I see it now; you look a lot like your mom."

That caught my attention. "You've met her?" I asked.

Petrina nodded. "Several times. They ate here a bit.

Most of the folks from the caravan park do." She glanced at the big white watch on her wrist. "In fact they'll probably dribble in anytime now."

"When was the last time you saw my mom and dad?" I asked.

Petrina cocked her head, studying me. "I heard rumors they were missing." She looked around and leaned forward as if to whisper something and I automatically leaned in to hear. "But I wasn't sure if that was another tall tale being bandied about to drum up tourism."

"Oh?"

"A lot of things get exaggerated in these parts. Copper pyramids anyone?" She scoffed, leaned back and focused on tucking her tank back into her jeans. "I mean, seriously. If there were a pyramid made of copper here, we'd have found it by now."

"Did my parents talk to you about that? The copper pyramid?"

She shrugged. "Sure, a time or two. I warned them you have to take a lot of those sorts of tales with a pinch of salt. That whole story started because someone figured the ABC range—that rock formation you see on the horizon—looks like the tail of a dragon and those spikes are the tail and that last one is the copper pyramid. But your folks seemed pretty smart. Your dad told me they were archeologists, so I figured they had their heads on straight."

"And you last saw them...?" I prompted again, for Petrina hadn't answered my initial question.

She tapped her chin, eyes focusing on something above my head. "Oh, let me see. A few days ago at least. They came in for dinner one day last week."

"Did they mention they were returning home?" I asked.

She shook her head, purple curls dancing over her shoulders. "Nope."

"And they didn't seem stressed or rushed or anything out of the ordinary?"

"Nope. They sat just over there." She pointed to a table by the window. "And had their heads real close together and whispered to each other all evening. They looked so sweet, obviously they still like each other." She winked and my lips twitched in a weak smile. Petrina continued, "So unusual to see that these days, more mature folks being sweet on each other. They are clearly in love, that's for sure. Even Kaylee noticed it and to get that girl to notice anything that doesn't revolve around taking her own photo and putting it up on Instagram is amazing."

Before I could ask who Kaylee was, a man called out from the pool table. "Hey, Petrina, two pale ales when you've got a minute!"

"Coming right up, Bluey," Petrina yelled back. "You two want to order any drinks while you sort out what you want to eat?" she said to us.

I shrugged. "Sure. How about a round of beers?"

"Tap's dry so it'll have to be a stubbie." Petrina nodded at the beer taps that had a cloth draped over them.

"That's fine." I had no idea what a stubbie was but figured I was about to find out.

"Any preference?" She jerked her thumb at the fridge behind her where an array of brown bottles was displayed. Ah. A stubbie was a bottle of beer. "Surprise us."

Petrina lined up five bottles of beer on the bar— the labels said Toohey's—and expertly popped the lids. "I'll start a tab for you. You can pay when you order your food."

"Thank you." Gran had already picked up two bottles and was heading back to the table when the front door opened and four people walked in.

"Here they come," Petrina said, nodding towards the newcomers, "These are your folks from Arrowstrand Caravan Park. That skinny piece of work at the front, that old man's name is Nigel. He's the guide for the caves. Those two strapping young fellas behind him are a couple of tourists he's been touting around for a week or so, and that..." She nodded at the young woman wearing daisy dukes, a low-cut tank that displayed her impressive double D's and cut off to display her flat abdomen, a spray tan you didn't get out of a bottle, long fake lashes and equally long fake nails. "That is Kaylee Webb, Andi and Colin's daughter. She helps behind the bar a few nights a week."

I watched the newcomers with interest. I was relatively sure one of these people had been responsible for breaking into my parents' trailer—because whoever it was, had used a key. There had been no signs of forced entry. Which meant they knew where the key was kept and had *borrowed* it, but then returned it; otherwise Andi would have noticed it missing. Unless it was Andi herself. And I hadn't ruled that out.

"The husband, Colin, he'll probably turn up later. He does a lot of sunset tours."

"Really?" That surprised me. There didn't seem to be that many visitors to warrant it. Petrina twigged straight away. "There's another town about fifty clicks down the road. He gets a lot of business there 'cos it's on the main highway. Arrowstrand is a destination type place. We don't get many visitors passing through. The caves are a big draw card, but the Webbs only started promoting the place as a tourism destination about three years ago, after the farm went belly up."

"Belly up?"

"Bankrupt. Well almost. Price of sheep dropped, getting next to nothing for the wool and the meat, they were struggling, but hanging in there. The fire was the straw that broke the camel's back."

"A fire?"

Petrina nodded. "The original homestead burned down a few years ago. Unsalvageable. They auctioned off what farm equipment they could, the government offered them some decent money for the land—with the plan to add it to the national forest around Wilpena Pound—and they agreed with the proviso they kept the land where the caves are. They've got about twenty acres. Enough money to build a new place, setup a caravan park, run the tours to the caves."

Kaylee, who'd tied an apron around her hips and joined Petrina behind the bar, interrupted us. "Who's this?" she asked, looking at me with interest.

"Rude much?" Petrina sighed shaking her head. "This is Harper. She's a guest at the caravan park, along with her friends over there." Petrina nodded toward the table where the others were watching us with interest. And that's when I realized I still had three bottles of beer in front of me.

"Lovely to meet you both." I smiled, scooping up the bottles by the neck. "I'd love to chat more later if that's okay?"

"Sure thing." Petrina smiled, wiping down the bar. "Anytime at all."

"You shouldn't listen to her," Kaylee snapped. "She's nothing but an old gossip and a busybody."

"Says you who's constantly listening in to everyone around her and posting about it on Instagram," Petrina snapped back, face tight. "Those tables need clearing." She nodded to the back of the room where the guys who were playing pool had set their empty glasses on a nearby table. Kaylee flounced away, an attitude in every step she took.

"I swear," Petrina muttered. "The older that girl gets the more the devil comes out in her. I don't know where she gets it from, not her mom, that's for sure. Andi is the sweetest, kindest person I've ever met. She deserves better than that brat of a daughter."

Raising one shoulder in an apologetic shrug I returned to the table, depositing the beers on the table.

"What was that all about?" Jenna asked, her eyes following Kaylee.

"Well, that is Kaylee, the daughter of the folks who run the trailer park," I explained. "And there's a wee bit of tension between her and the bartender, Petrina, by the looks of things."

Remy chuckled. "I remember being that young and thinking I knew everything there was to know. And that my *elders* were a bunch of idiots."

"Me too," Jenna said sheepishly. "I was so mean to my mom when I was a teenager."

I thought about my relationship with my mother, the days I would snap at her because I thought she was being unfair, uncool. Now I'd give anything to have her sitting at the table with us where I could tell her how much I love her. I'd thought I had all the time in the world but now I had an ominous feeling time was running out.

"Set 'em up, hot stuff!"

I rubbed a weary hand over my eyes, resigned to the fact that Gran was at it again. Hustling the men at pool. So far, she was fifty dollars up. To be fair, she had an unfair advantage, in that these poor unsuspecting country folk were not expecting the eyeful they got when Gran draped herself over the table. Those in front got the cleavage shot, those behind, the rear end shot where her dress rode up to indecent heights.

"Come on, Gran," I interrupted before she could fleece them of even more of their hard-earned money. "It's been a long day. Aren't you tired?"

"Where's your stamina, girl?" Gran beamed at me, cheeks flushed. "It's morning in Whitefall Cove and I'm on Whitefall Cove time." So was I, which was why

I felt like I'd been awake for twenty-four hours and my eyeballs had been rolled in sand. By all intents and purposes Gran should be sound asleep by now. I couldn't fathom how the brief nap she'd had this afternoon had revived her so much. I narrowed my eyes, studying the rosy cheeks and sparkling eyes. *Oh, that little sneak.* She'd cast a spell. I wish I'd thought of it!

My attention was diverted from Gran when one of the men Petrina had pointed out earlier as staying at the trailer park stepped up to the table, placing a twenty-dollar bill down. "I'm game," he said, his voice carrying a thick accent.

"Sure thing, sugar." Gran winked at him, spent an inordinate amount of time chalking the end of her queue before suggestively blowing the excess blue powder off. "What's your name, honey?"

"I'm Tamir." He grinned in return, his teeth white against his tanned skin.

"Tamir. Interesting name." Gran nodded. "Where you from, Tamir?"

"Croatia, ma'am." Tamir set up the billiard balls and grabbed a cue.

"Pft, none of that ma'am stuff, thank you very much. Call me Alice." Gran popped a hip against the table and eyeballed the young man who had to be late twenties, maybe thirty.

Tamir laughed and nodded his head. "Okay... Alice.

I've been watching you. Your winning streak is about to end."

Gran barked a laugh. "Is it now, young whippersnapper?" Tapping her fingers against her pool cue, she narrowed her eyes at him. "I love a challenge. Let's see what you've got."

Tamir gave Gran a run for her money, but in the end gracefully admitted defeat. Throughout the game, Gran had grilled him on his life story. He had traveled to Australia with his friend Omar two weeks ago. They'd spent time in Sydney, before traveling to Adelaide then out to Arrowstrand. The pair of them were treasure hunters. Gran had flicked a quick glance my way when Tamir had revealed that bit of information. His friend Omar was sitting opposite, watching the game. He had the same olive skin and dark eyes as Tamir, but instead of a head full of thick black hair that Tamir sported, Omar's hair was cropped close to his skull. Nigel, the wiry tour guide, stopped by a time or two and he and Omar disappeared into the beer garden at the rear of the hotel to smoke, coming back reeking of nicotine.

Kaylee sashayed over, a tray balanced against her hip as she collected empty glasses. My eyes narrowed when she passed by Tamir and her hand trailed over his thigh. His dark eyes followed her every move.

"Do you work here every night?" I asked her.

"Nope," she replied without looking at me. "Three,

maybe four nights, depending on how busy they get and what other plans I have on."

"You wouldn't be hinting at your birthday, would you?" Tamir teased her, and she fluttered her lashes at him.

"Now why would you think that, handsome?"

"Oh, because you've dropped about a billion hints this week." He chuckled, then told us, "Kaylee turns twenty-one this week."

"In three days, actually. The twenty-sixth."

"That's a blood moon," Gran said. I looked at her in surprise. I hadn't known that.

"What's that?" Kaylee asked, head tilted.

"It's a lunar eclipse," Gran answered. "It can have a significant impact on your spiritual and astrological sides."

Kaylee stared hard at Gran for a moment before shrugging one shoulder. "If you believe in that sort of thing."

Gran inclined her head. "Do you?"

"Do I what?"

"Believe in that sort of thing?"

Seconds ticked by as we waited for Kaylee to answer. "No. I don't." She finally said and moved away to continue clearing glasses.

"Shame." Gran picked up her beer and drained it. "Okay fellas, I think I need to get the granddaughter home to bed. She looks as if a stiff breeze could blow her over." Gran laid her cue on the table.

"Oh, don't stop on my account," I mocked, but stood, keen to get back to the trailer and try to connect with Mom and Dad via astral walking. We stopped by the table where Remy and Blake had been engrossed in conversation all evening—I figured they had a lot to catch up on but was a little put out he hadn't paid me much attention to me this evening. Again, I wasn't sure what I was expecting from him, but I felt like one minute he blew hot, the other cold, and I didn't know what to make of it.

"We're ready to go if you are?" I said to them both.

Remy stood up immediately. "Oh God, it's ten o'clock. You guys must be so exhausted. I'm sorry, I should have wrapped this up earlier."

I smiled and patted her arm. "It's okay. Gran was having fun and we got to know some of our fellow travelers, it's all good."

"Where's Jenna?" Blake asked, pushing his chair in beneath the table.

"I think she's outside taking a call," Remy answered, leading the way to the door.

Outside, the air was cool enough to make you shiver, a pleasant change from the heat of the day. Crickets chirped loudly, the only sound in the night air, aside from Jenna's voice. She was pacing back and forth as she talked on the phone. From the snippets that reached my ears I figured she was talking to the editor of the *Whitefall Cove Tribune*, finalizing a story. Seeing us standing on the footpath, she quickly wrapped up the call and joined us.

Piling into the Range Rover, we traveled back to the trailer park in silence, each lost in our own thoughts. I was keen to connect with Mom and Dad. I'd been trying every night since I learned they'd gone missing, but so far, nothing. Now I was in Australia, and closer to them physically, I hoped to finally connect. Then it was just a matter of rescuing them from whatever predicament they found themselves in.

"Can I walk you to your trailer?" Blake asked when we pulled up at the park.

"Sure." A little thrill went through me at the prospect of being alone with him. I was all over the place with how I felt about this man. One minute I wanted to fully explore a relationship with him, the next I wanted to back away. He was full of secrets and bad boy vibes that set off my radar, and having recently been hurt by my cheating ex-fiancé Simon, I was not in the market to have my heart trampled on by another man. And let's not forget the crush I had on Whitefall Cove Detective Jackson Ward. My love life had gotten more complicated since returning home.

I could feel the heat of Blake's hand where he placed it against my lower back to guide me across the park to where my parents' trailer sat.

"Just let Bandit out when you get there," Remy called. "I'll whistle for him."

Craning my neck over my shoulder, I could just make out her silhouette in the doorway of her cabin. "Will do."

The walk across the packed earth to my front door was all too short, and we made it in silence. Finally, I blurted out, "What are you thinking?"

His reply surprised me. "That you look beautiful in the moonlight."

I tripped over my own feet at his words. "I do?" I squeaked, feeling a warm tingle spread through my bones. Gah, I was such a sucker for compliments. Was I that needy that all it took was a man to say something nice and I melted into a puddle at his feet?

"You do," he murmured. We'd reached my door, and I turned to look up at him in the darkness. Before I could say a word, he lowered his head and my eyes fluttered closed, face tilted in anticipation of his kiss. Only the kiss didn't happen. He briefly rested his forehead against mine, before dragging in a ragged breath and stepping back.

"Blake?" The word slipped out before I could stop it, an echo of the chaos ricocheting around in my skull.

"I'm sorry," he said. "It's complicated."

"Complicated?" My voice went up an octave or two. "Complicated as in you have a wife? A girlfriend?

Significant other?" Was he no better than lying cheating Simon? Life couldn't be that unfair, surely?

He shook his head, mouth grim. "None of those things."

I opened my mouth to demand answers but didn't get the chance. "Goodnight, Harper." And he was gone, disappearing into the night.

I stood there, mouth agape, shocked beyond words. Shutting my mouth with a snap, I opened the trailer door. Bandit bounded out. "Go back to your mom." I told him, blocking Archie from following with my foot. "Oh, no you don't, mister. No nocturnal wanderings for you."

Meow?

"Sorry, buddy," I leaned down and scratched behind his ears as I locked the trailer door. "Not tonight."

Mrrrow. Meow, meow, meeeeow. I chuckled at Archie's noises. "I know you want to go out and play and explore. Just not tonight, okay? I want to try to contact Mom and Dad and... I might need you." He seemed to accept that explanation since he immediately stopped his chirping and complaining and rubbed around my legs with a purr, as if he understood the angst burning through my veins. Confusion over my feelings for Blake, worry over my parents. And exhaustion from traveling around the globe to get here and find them.

Blowing out a breath, I slipped off my shoes and climbed onto the bed, sitting in the center cross-legged. Archie jumped up and climbed into the cradle my legs made, turned around in a circle before finally settling with a soft purr. Closing my eyes, I ran my fingers through his soft fur.

"Let's do this," I whispered. Concentrating my magic, I searched for a connection to Mom, a thread I could follow. I was here, sitting on the bed she'd slept in, in the trailer she'd lived in. Surely, I could find a trailing ember of her essence to latch onto and follow. Yet I found nothing.

I didn't even know I was crying until I felt the sandpaper lick of Archie's tongue on my chin. Quickly swiping my fingers over my cheeks to wipe away the moisture, I looked down into his golden eyes. "Sorry, boy," I sniffed. "Didn't mean to drip all over you." He head butted my chin, and I hugged him. "Why can't I find her, Archie? Why can't I connect? I mean, the obvious answer is because she's dead—they both are —but I'd know it. Gran would know it. It's almost as if they are in a bubble, cut off from us."

Meow... meow.

"I won't give up. I'll keep trying. Maybe in the caves I'll have more luck?"

Lying down, I dragged the covers over myself and closed my eyes. Sleep claimed me quickly. A deep dark sleep I eventually woke from with a start. Sitting up, hand to my thundering heart, I glanced around. Archie was meowing at the door and scratching at it. Sunlight poured through the windows where I'd forgotten to draw the curtains the night before.

"Okay, okay. You can go outside." Climbing out of bed, I crossed to the door. "But no wandering off, okay? Stay where I can see you. And don't play with anything that has fangs or venom. Understand?"

Meow.

Opening the door, I let him out, before hurrying through a shower and then a breakfast of toast and coffee. I was grateful Mom and Dad already had supplies in. I was brushing my hair and pulling it up into a ponytail when Archie scratched at the door to come back in.

"Back so soon?" I held open the door for him, not noticing he was dragging something inside with him until he dropped it on my foot. The scream that involuntarily left my throat was long and loud. He'd brought me a dead bird.

"Oh, Archie, you didn't kill it, did you?" I nudged it with my foot, only then noticing the black feathers were covered in blood. It was one of the native crows, similar to a raven.

Archie meowed in what I considered to be an outraged tone. Okay, so he didn't kill it. It couldn't have died of natural causes, too much blood for that. Even as it lay on the floor blood pooled beneath it and my stomach turned. Turning to the door that still stood open, I staggered outside and sucked in a breath of fresh air.

Blake was running across the park. "What is it?" he yelled, "What's happened? I heard you scream!"

I pointed a shaking hand to my trailer. "Dead bird."

He reached me, briefly touched my cheek before peering inside. "Sure is," he muttered. "That's a lot of blood."

"That's what I thought." I kept my back to the door, not wanting to see the dead bird again.

"Did Archie do it?" Blake asked.

Archie wound his way around my feet, protesting his innocence. I shook my head. "Archie doesn't kill wildlife."

"You sure about that? He's a cat, after all. It's what they do."

"He's also my familiar. He doesn't need to hunt. You're going to have to trust me—my cat did not do this."

I risked a glance over my shoulder. Blake was leaning into the trailer, examining the bird. "You're right. No cat did this. In fact, no animal did this."

"What do you mean?"

"Someone has cut this bird's throat. With a sharp instrument."

My stomach lurched, and I almost brought up my breakfast. "What?" I gasped.

"There's something else." His voice sounded ominous. Did I even want to know? Seemed I didn't have a choice for Blake kept on talking. "There's dark magic involved. I can feel it. Someone killed this animal as part of a spell or hex."

"You're sure?"

"Touch it. See for yourself."

"I really don't want to," I muttered, yet found myself drawn forward and reaching out a trembling hand. I tentatively touched a silky black feather, my heart aching for this poor creature. As soon as we connected, I felt it, a wave of energy, dark and foreboding. I snatched my hand away as if burned. "Oh, that is *dark*." I gasped. "Is it? Is it... *black* magic?" I whispered. I'd never dealt in black magic before. It was taboo. Forbidden.

"What's happening?" Jenna and Remy joined us. Blake slung an arm around my shoulders and drew me away from the doorway so they could see inside.

Jenna immediately pulled out her phone and took photos. I looked at her incredulously.

"What?" she said defensively. "I'm documenting the evidence. The way you two are acting this isn't some random animal kill. And despite the amount of blood, this didn't happen here. Archie?"

I nodded. "Not in the way you think. Archie didn't

kill it. He must have found it, brought it home. Although goodness knows how. It's almost the same size as him."

Remy waited until Jenna moved out of the way before inspecting the bird for herself. "You feel it?" she asked Blake, who nodded grimly.

"Feel what?" Jenna asked, typing notes into her phone.

"Black magic." The three of us said in unison.

"Seriously? I can't feel it."

"It's masked, but there. Touch it," Blake told her. "Physical contact may help."

Jenna reached back in, then quickly snatched her hand back not unlike what I'd done a few minutes earlier. "Oh my God, you're right. That's foul. No pun intended."

Blake and Remy had their heads bent close together, whispering, and Jenna looked at me with eyebrows raised. I shrugged. I had no idea.

Remy straightened and cleared her throat. "Blake and I will take care of this." She tilted her head to indicate the dead crow. "Harper, you need to drop into the police station to update them on your parents' situation. How do you feel about driving in? Think you can handle it?"

"I don't mind going with her." Jenna jumped in before I could answer. "I'll drive. Unless you want to?" she added.

I shook my head. "Happy for you to drive, Jen." I wasn't at all confident I could cope with driving on the wrong side of the road.

Blake rested his hand on my shoulder, bringing my attention back to him. "We'll keep an eye on Gran and Archie. You focus on finding your parents. We'll deal with this."

There was a lot of *we* in that sentence and none of it referred to him and me. I glanced from him to Remy and back again. Was there something going on between them that I needed to be concerned about? They seemed close, but I put that down to the fact that Blake's and Remy's bosses were friends, that they were friends too. But now I had a niggling suspicion something more was going on. Yet last night he said he wasn't involved with anyone else. But there was more to their relationship than mere friendship. I was determined to find out what. But it would have to wait. Right now I needed to find out what the police knew about my parents' disappearance.

CHAPTER
FIVE

"Yeah, mate, all good.... nah, nah, don't be a drongo."

"What's a drongo?" I whispered to Jenna as we waited at the counter of the police station. The one and only officer, dressed in a navy-blue uniform, was on the phone, although he'd acknowledged us with a nod when we came in.

"I have no idea," Jenna mumbled back, her eyes intent on the officer.

"Catch ya later, Bluey." The officer hung up and stood, making his way to the counter. "What can I help you with, ladies?"

"I'm Harper Jones," I introduced myself. "I believe there's a missing persons report for my parents, Judith and Keith Jones?"

"Ah yes!" He snapped his fingers and swiveled on

his heel to return to his desk where he rifled through the papers in a tray on the corner. "Thanks for coming in, Harper," he said, eyes skimming over the file in his hand. "All the way from America. That's quite a trip."

"Yeah."

"And you are?" He turned his attention to Jenna.

"Jenna Owens, a journalist for the *Whitefall Cove Tribune*."

His face registered shock before he quickly schooled his features. "Fair dinkum? You brought the press?"

"What?" I looked from him to Jenna and back again, then shook my head. "No, no. Jenna is my best friend. She's here for support."

"But if it turns out there's a story here, that'll be good too." Jenna grinned. His eyes roamed over her, giving her a thorough inspection from the top of her head to the tip of her toes and the slight curl of his mouth told me he liked what he saw. A quick glance at Jenna and the flush of color in her cheeks told me the admiration was mutual.

"Righto then. I'm Senior Sergeant Mick Gould. Call me Mick. Come on through to the interview room and we'll go over the official part and I'll fill you in on where I'm at with the investigation."

It turned out the investigation had turned up little. In fact, it had turned up nothing. Mick had an APB out on my parents' car—it hadn't been seen since leaving the caravan park the night they supposedly left. He'd put calls through to all the gas stations between Arrowstrand and Adelaide, put in a request for CCTV and plate recognition software to be run in and around Adelaide airport, but no trace of them or their four-wheel drive. Mick seemed confident they hadn't left the area, that it was most likely a simple explanation of them forgetting to inform us of a change in plans and that they were, in fact, camping off site somewhere.

I'd had to sign paperwork, provided him with a recent photo of Mom and Dad, and then we were free to go.

Outside the police station Jenna grinned at me. "He was hot."

I snorted. "Yeah, I noticed the two of you checking each other out."

"I love his accent." Jenna sighed, climbing into the cab of the Land Rover.

"What? Australian? You sure it's got nothing to do with the fact you're a sucker for a man in uniform?" I teased settling myself into the passenger side and clipping my seatbelt into place.

"That too." She giggled. "Can you imagine being the only cop for hundreds of miles? Responsible for all of this?" She waved a hand, indicating the street we were parked on and the land beyond.

"Nope, I truly can't," I conceded. "It's a big job."

"We'll find them." Jenna sobered, patting my knee before turning the key in the ignition. "Between Remy and her bureau, your magic, and the local police, something will turn up."

"Yeah, I know." Putting on a brave face, I smiled. "So, let's go explore these caves then. Remy and Blake should have gotten rid of the crow by now."

Jenna frowned. "That crow business was so weird. Who could be using magic around here? And why?"

It hit me then, why I hadn't been able to forge a connection with my parents and I gasped. "What is it?" Jenna swiveled her head to look at me as we turned off the main street and onto the track back to the trailer park. "Are you okay?"

"Magic," I said. "Someone is using magic to hide my parents. I've been trying to astral-walk ever since we found out they were missing, and nothing. It's like they don't exist. I thought for sure I'd be able to connect with them once we were here, and I tried again last night, but again, nothing. But now it makes sense. I should have thought of it sooner, but I never considered someone could use magic to hide them."

"Are there covens in these parts?" Jenna asked. "Any way we can find out who practices magic?"

I shrugged. "I have no idea. I wonder if there's some sort of register for covens. I guess I could put a call in to Drixworths and see what they know? Although I'm not keen to alert them to the fact I'm involved with something involving dark magic." I'd already had my witch's license suspended once for using magic to harm humans.

"Couldn't you say you think it involves magic and do they know if there's a coven here? If there are witches here? I didn't sense any other paranormals at the hotel last night, but that's not to say they're not here."

"True. And Remy might have a way of outing them using some of her snazzy equipment." Hope bloomed in my chest. Archie finding the dead bird may have been the breakthrough we needed.

"Bad news I'm afraid," Remy told us when we returned to the park. "Our guide, Nigel, had a booking he'd forgotten to tell Andi about."

"So, he's not available to take us to the caves?" Damn. I'd been hoping to visit Mom and Dad's worksite today.

"It's all a bit suss really." Remy screwed up her nose. "Apparently Tamir and Omar booked him last night at the hotel."

"But they've been to the caves before." Jenna planted her hands on her hips, ready for an argument. "Why would they need a guide now? I bet it's because we're here. They think we're going to swoop in and steal any treasure out from under them."

"Okay, okay." Blake stepped in before Jenna could get any more wound up. "Let's not jump to conclusions. The upshot is, Nigel and the two treasure hunters left at dawn. There's nothing we can do about that now. The way I see it, we have two options."

"Which are?" Jenna demanded, still seething they had stolen our guide out from under us at the last moment.

"We go by ourselves, with no guide. Or we wait until Nigel is available. Because they left early this morning, Andi thinks Nigel may be back around lunchtime or early afternoon. But to cover our bases, Andi has booked us with him again tomorrow."

Andi, who'd stepped out to join us when she heard us return, had a baby sling tied around her waist and shoulders and her hands ran over the small bundle supported inside. "I'm so sorry this happened. I'd really prefer it if you didn't go to the caves on your own, not for the first time at least. They are a vast network of interlocking tunnels and caverns that go on for miles and it would be so easy to get lost. Nigel has maps and local knowledge that is invaluable."

She was right. It was too dangerous to go alone, and I opened my mouth to agree with her when a baby kangaroo popped its head out from the sling and looked at us.

"Oh, my gosh!" Jenna squealed, rushing forward, then quickly dropping her voice to a whisper. "I'm sorry, little fella," she breathed. "Did I startle you?"

"This is Joey." Andi moved more of the fabric aside to reveal the small kangaroo. "A car hit his mother. The driver found Joey in her pouch and brought him to me to raise."

"That is amazing." I joined Jenna, holding out my hand for Joey to sniff and then giving his fur a stroke.

"Do you release him into the wild when he's grown up?" Jenna asked.

Andi shook her head. "No, he'll be too used to hanging out with us humans. But he will have free rein of this place and he'll wander and explore, but he'll keep coming back. He'll know there is food here."

"You've done this before?" Blake took a turn fussing over the tiny creature, its head looking impossibly tiny next to his large hand.

"Many times. You'll see roos come through the caravan park from time to time. Most of them are ones I hand reared." Joey fussed, burying his face back into the sling and wriggling around. "He's hungry. Time for another bottle." She tucked the fabric over his head, concealing him. "Sorry again about the mix-up. I should have called Nigel on his mobile last night when you made the booking, but I assumed he would have checked in the office first this morning."

"That's okay," Remy said. "Mix-ups happen. But

yes, if we can absolutely make sure he's available for us tomorrow that would be wonderful, thank you."

Gran cut in, changing the subject entirely, "How did it go with the cops?"

"Nothing new," I said, while Jenna quickly added, "You would have liked Senior Sergeant Mick Gould, Gran."

Gran's face split into a huge smile. "Dishy was he?"

"Extremely." Jenna nodded with an exaggerated wink. I couldn't contain my eye roll. I wasn't sure who was worse, Gran or Jenna! Then I noticed what Gran was wearing. A hot pink mesh tunic over a yellow bikini. And Ugg boots. Purple, but no bedazzling this time.

"Interesting outfit."

"Thank you." Gran curtsied. "I thought I'd take a dip in the swimming hole while you lot explore the caves, but since you're not going, maybe we could all take a dip."

"Are there crocodiles? Or is it alligators?" Blake asked Andi.

"Neither. Not even eels," Andi replied. "All you'll find in there are yabbies. Great for cooling off in. You're welcome to take a dip anytime."

"What's a yabby?" I asked, worried Gran was in danger of being bitten by something nasty.

"Crayfish," Remy supplied, then held up her finger and thumb. "Small ones."

"I might join you later, Gran. I need to put in a call to Drixworths. And we"—I indicated Jenna, Remy, and Blake—"need to decide what our next move will be."

Gran flipped a striped towel over her shoulder and hurried off toward the swimming hole, calling "Toodles" and giving us a wave over her shoulder as she left. Archie and Bandit trotted after her.

"Traitors." Remy chuckled, not in the least concerned that her dog had abandoned her to go swimming with Gran.

"Does Bandit like the water?" I asked, cocking my head and watching until they disappeared from view.

"Loves it. He'll be in before your Gran has even reached it. How about Archie? Is he a water cat?"

"Not that I know of."

Andi bid us farewell, returning to the house to feed Joey. As soon as she was out of earshot I asked, "What did you find out? About the dead crow? Did you find where it was killed? And who killed it?"

"No. Just that it was tainted with dark magic. I'd say someone killed it for its blood."

I sucked in a breath. "Blood magic then. That is dark." A shiver wracked me despite the heat. "And you couldn't trace where it had come from?"

"We followed a blood trail of sorts, leading to a bin by the back of the house," Remy said. "We think Archie may have found the bird there."

"So, whoever is practicing magic—dark or

otherwise—has to be staying here in the trailer park," Jenna said, and Remy nodded.

"We should ward the trailer and your cabins," I said.

Blake nodded. "Good idea. But let's wait until nightfall. Don't want to tip our hand that we're onto them. We'll ward under the cover of darkness."

"I'm going to do some more research on the copper pyramid," Remy said. "See if I can find the thread your parents found and give it a tug, see what unravels."

"Great idea." Jenna piped up, "I'm going to write this up. There's a story here, I know it."

Before Blake spoke, I grabbed his arm. "Actually, could you help me with something?"

His eyebrows shot up. "Yeah of course."

Bidding farewell to Remy and Jenna, he followed me into the trailer where I busied myself putting a pot of coffee on.

"What's up?" he asked, making himself comfortable at the diner-style booth seating. I told him my theory about Mom and Dad being hidden by magic. He listened in silence, tapping a finger on the table as I spoke.

When I finished, he looked at me with his piercing dark eyes. "Sounds plausible," he finally said, and I almost sagged with relief. "So, what do you need my help with?"

"Well, I thought we could combine our powers?

That maybe that would give me enough of a boost to bust through whatever spell has them hidden."

"Combining our powers could be risky. I'm fae, not a witch. Our powers might not mesh well."

"We managed okay when that orb was attacking us back in Whitefall Cove," I pointed out, but he was already shaking his head.

"That was different. I wasn't combining my magic with yours. I was using my magic alongside you. A double pronged attack."

"Oh." I turned my back and fiddled with the coffee cups, wishing the damn machine would hurry up.

"But I guess it can't hurt to try," he added, and I spun to face him, hands clasped to my chest.

"Really?"

"Why not? This is our first strong lead; we should do everything it takes to find your parents and if that means experimenting with our own powers..." And that's when I hesitated.

The way he said it. Experimenting with our powers. Pretty sure that was against my probation with Drixworths Academy of Witchcraft and Wizardry. I'd lost my witch's license last year for harming a human with magic—in my defense it hadn't been intentional. When I'd caught my fiancé cheating on me with a student at the university where he worked, my magic had sort of exploded out of me and I'd changed him into a monkey. And then a rat.

Then a snake. Of course, I'd changed him back to human, but the damage had been done and I'd lost my license. Then I'd lost my job. It was a given that I'd lost my fiancé. I'd packed up my car and moved back to Whitefall Cove that same day.

"Regrets already?" Blake asked, one dark brow arching.

I shrugged. "No."

He laughed. "You're such a bad liar."

I gave him a tight smile but said nothing, instead turned my attention back to the coffee, pouring us both a cup. As I slid Blake's across to the table he asked, "Was anything missing?"

"What?"

"When you tidied up the trailer, was anything missing?"

"Oh. Ummm. I didn't really check. I just kinda shoved everything back where it belonged." And now I was kicking myself that I hadn't thought to see if whoever had searched the trailer had taken anything. I was saved from further beating myself up by my phone ringing.

"Jackson?" I hadn't expected to hear from Detective Jackson Ward. Not when I was all the way in Australia, and he was back home in Whitefall Cove. "Has something happened?"

"No, no, it's all good here," he reassured me and I

sagged with relief. For a minute I thought he was ringing with more bad news.

"So...what's up?" I asked. Blake watched me with those mesmerizing dark eyes of his and I almost felt guilty for talking with Jackson in his presence. I'd had a crush on Jackson ever since I'd returned to Whitefall Cove, only Jackson was dating fellow police officer Liliana Miles. Jackson was also a necromancer, and we'd discovered that whenever we were together in my bookstore, The Dusty Attic, the ghost of my high school nemesis Whitney Sims would appear for all to see—and hear. It made for interesting conversations, and since I didn't particularly like ghosts, Jackson thought it a hoot to drop into the shop unannounced purely to amuse himself at my reaction to Whitney.

"Oh, nothing. I just wanted to check in, see how you're doing?"

"Oh." Blinking twice in surprise, I filled him in on what we'd discovered so far. Which wasn't a lot.

"Blake's with you now?" Jackson's voice turned sharp, and I rolled my eyes. The two men had some alpha male rivalry going on and I didn't have time for their egos.

"Yes. Look I've got to go. Thanks for your call, Jackson. Say hi to Liliana for me." I hung up and placed my phone down on the table a little too hard.

Blake grinned. "Trouble in paradise?"

"Shut up," I grumbled. Blake had been teasing me for a while now that Jackson had the hots for me. I didn't see it. And I wondered how I'd gotten myself into this bizarre triangle of liking two men yet unsure of either of their feelings towards me. Or motives. Jackson was spoken for. And Blake was a mystery wrapped in an enigma and I feared that was partly why I found him so attractive. He was a puzzle I wanted to solve. But I also feared he would break my heart, and having it so thoroughly stomped on by Simon mere months ago, I wasn't sure I was ready to risk it again.

We sat in silence and drank our coffee, my mind a furious whirl of anxiety. Find my parents. Sort out my love life— or lack thereof. What happened to the quiet life I'd planned for myself in Whitefall Cove?

"Are you sure you want to do this? Because you don't look sure," Blake said, sitting across from me in the tiny kitchen of the trailer.

"I am absolutely, positively sure," I replied with a firm nod of my head. I needed the reassurance of connecting with my mom, to know that she was alive —Dad too—once and for all. It was the not knowing that was eating away at me and despite the *I'm doing fine* face I was presenting to the world, the truth was I was scared to death I may not see my parents again.

Blake sighed like he wasn't convinced, but he went along with it, anyway.

"I've no idea how to do this," he told me. "Any suggestions?"

"How about I try to astral-walk like I do normally but you..." I trailed off.

"I what?" he pressed.

"Touch me," I blurted. "We'd need a physical connection for this to work. So, touch me. Hold my hand. Then focus on channeling your magic into me."

"So, I'd be using you as a conduit?"

"More like I'd be using you. But it doesn't matter. We just need enough oomph to break through whatever spell is hiding them."

"If it's a spell," he pointed out.

"Can you at least pretend to be positive?" I grumbled, my stress levels rising.

"Sorry. You're right. Okay, let's do this."

"Ummm." I didn't know how to word my next request without it coming out the wrong way.

"Just spit it out, Harper." Blake sighed, knowing me all too well.

"Okay, I like to do this on the bed. Sitting up!" I quickly added, lest he think this was some nefarious plan to get him into bed. "Cross-legged. On the bed."

He stood up and moved to the bed. "I can do that." Toeing off his shoes, he climbed onto the bed and positioned himself cross-legged, leaving enough space for me to join him. I followed suit, flicking off my shoes and crawling into position. I sucked in a deep breath, rolled my shoulders and blew out the breath, closing my eyes and centering myself. Without opening my eyes, I held out my hands, jumped a little at the hot sizzle that shot up my arms when Blake clasped my hands in his.

Then I focused on finding my parents. Or more specifically my mom, since she was the one who was a witch. Dad was human. Which was strange then that I'd have such powerful magic, given my diluted bloodline, but nevertheless, Drixworths had assured me I was a powerful witch and they'd given me a familiar, Archie, to help me control and channel my magic. I wondered now if I should have Archie with us to help, but it was too late. I already felt like I was zooming down a superhighway, traveling beyond the speed of light through memory trails of my mom. Then, with an audible pop, there she was, right in front of me.

"Harper." Her smile was everything I remembered, and I smiled back at her, so full of relief I couldn't speak. She wrapped her arms around me and hugged me tight and I breathed in the scent that was purely Mom.

"Are you okay?" I asked, my voice wavering. "Is Dad with you?"

"We're both fine," she reassured me, but then her image flickered, like an old movie on videotape.

"Mom?" She shimmered and crackled. She was speaking, but I couldn't make out the words. She clasped my hands in hers and I heard the word *geospiral* before—*snap*, she was gone.

My eyes popped open, and I stared into the dark pools of Blake's eyes. "Did you see that?" I whispered. He nodded, dazed.

"Did you hear what she said? All I really got was that they're being held somewhere. I couldn't see where, but it was dark. And the word geospiral. You?"

He opened his mouth to speak, nothing came out, so he cleared his throat and tried again. "Same," he croaked.

"Are you okay?"

"I think I need a cup of tea." He let go of my hands to run his fingers through his hair and that was when I noted the pasty hue beneath his tan.

"Tea? Since when do you drink tea?" I asked, waiting for my own stomach to settle down.

"I'm fine." Swinging his legs off the bed, he scooped his boots up and hurried to the door.

"Blake? You're acting a little weird," I said, hopping off the bed and following him to the door. "Are you sure you're okay?"

He fled without looking back and I stood watching him, puzzled. Did he feel ill and didn't want me to see him hurl? But it was his words that had me frowning. Asking for a cup of tea. I'd never seen him drink tea. I was sure I'd heard him tell Gran that he only drank coffee. How bizarre.

Brushing aside the strange episode with Blake, I focused on what my mom had said—

geospiral. Hadn't Remy talked about geospirals on the way to Arrowstrand? Sitting on the front step of the trailer, I pulled my shoes back on and watched Blake as he made his way back to his cabin. I felt bad he felt unwell, but happy that I'd busted through whatever spell had been cast. Jumping up, I hurried over to Remy's cabin and knocked on the door. She opened it almost immediately.

"Hey, come on in." She opened the door wide, and I stepped inside, surprised to see Jenna sitting at the kitchen table, laptop open in front of her, furiously typing.

"Hi, Harper. Come to join the fun?" Jenna glanced at me, but her fingers kept flying across the keyboard. Remy had her own industrial-looking laptop open on the table with a stack of books and paperwork piled next to it. She moved them aside. "Come sit." She smiled.

"What do you know about geospirals?" I asked her, pulling out one of the kitchen chairs and taking a seat.

"Geospirals are basically a circular pattern etched or painted into rocks," Remy said. "Why?"

"Because with Blake's help I managed to astral-walk and connect with my mom. We only had seconds together, but she and Dad are okay. Alive. Then we lost the connection and I could only make out one word. Geospirals."

"Get outta town!" Jenna slapped her laptop shut

and grabbed my hand across the tabletop. "That's wonderful news, Harper."

My smile was wide. "Agreed."

Remy was puzzling over what I'd told them. "Do you think I could look at your parents' notes? That might help with context."

"Absolutely. Mom always journaled about their adventures and there's a ton of maps and journals in Dad's old chest in the trailer."

"You don't mind?" Remy was already gathering up her laptop, shoving it into her satchel along with a notebook and pencil.

"Of course not. It would make more sense to you than it would to me."

"Good thinking." Jenna stood, tucking her laptop under her arm. "I'm coming too."

Together we traipsed back across the park to the trailer. I hefted the chest out of the closet and onto the bed, opening the lid.

"Wow!" Remy breathed. "This is amazing." She removed journal after journal, stacked them one atop the other, placed the maps on their own separate pile.

"Anything we can do to help?" Jenna asked.

Remy nodded. "They were both meticulous note takers. Can you sort these into date order? We'll work our way backwards."

"Do you think they found the copper pyramid?" I

asked, handing Jenna a handful of the books and picking up the remaining ones for myself.

Remy shrugged. "It's possible. Or should I say, nothing is impossible. It's good news that your mom got a message to you, Harper. Now we have something to work with."

"Yeah well, the word geospirals doesn't tell us a lot," I grumbled.

"It doesn't tell you much, but it could tell me a lot," Remy pointed out, pausing in her rummaging of the chest to shoot me a sharp look. "How about you freshen up that coffee pot? This could take a while."

Three hours later Remy softly closed the notebook she'd been reading and laid her hand on the cover. Jenna and I had made quick work of the other journals, all of them pre-dating the trip to Arrowstrand. That left one journal for Remy to devour and make sense of. In the meantime, Jenna and I had found an old pack of cards in the chest and were playing Rummy.

"I think I have something," Remy said.

"Oh?" I glanced from her to my hand of cards and back again. Remy looked excited.

"What did you find?" Jenna asked, placing her cards facedown on the table.

"The geospirals are a language. An ancient language. Your dad has started to decode it." She picked up the journal and flicked to a page, holding it out for me to see. A bunch of swirly squiggles. "Okay."

Despite growing up with archeologists, I didn't know all that much about their craft. The swirly squiggles were simply swirly squiggles to me.

"Also, I think they hid something here."

That got my attention. I sat up straight and looked around. "Hid something? What? It would have to be small."

"They found some geospirals etched into rock. Small. Pebble sized."

"Let's get searching!" Jenna was already up and out of her seat.

I stood, hands on hips, and surveyed the trailer. Where would my parents hide a pebble? "Is it just one?" I asked Remy.

"Possibly two or three."

"And how big are we talking? A big pebble? Or small pebble?"

She held out her hand, pointing to her thumb. "I'd say about the size of my thumbnail."

We searched the trailer from top to bottom. Nothing. Jenna was in the bathroom, shaking every bottle of shampoo and lotion. Remy had her nose buried in the journal again, while I went through the pantry—it was the only place we hadn't looked. Every open canister or package I stuck a fork in and swirled it around, feeling for the telltale clunk of an unexpected stone in the contents. Murphy's Law it was the very last thing I'd checked, and at this point I thought Remy was mistaken and nothing was hidden here at all when the container of rice I was idly stirring with the fork made a twang as the tines hit something solid. Remy's head shot up, and I looked down at the plastic container in my hand in shock.

"You found it!" Remy jumped up, ditching the journal and snatching the container from my hands. Holding it over the sink, she plunged her hand in and felt around.

"Gross. I'm not eating that now you've had your hands in it," I said, watching with bated breath. Jenna joined us, sucking in a breath when Remy held up a smooth pebble between her finger and thumb. We leaned closer.

"It has those circles on it," I said.

Remy nodded, carefully placed the pebble on the countertop, and continued searching. All up there were four. They all looked the same to me, but Remy pointed out the miniscule differences in the circles etched into the surface of the tiny rocks. "See? The distance between the lines is different, and the circles on this one are almost perfectly round, but on this one they are more oval shaped."

"And that means?" Jenna asked, snapping photos with her phone.

"I'm not one hundred percent sure yet," Remy admitted. "But it was obviously something important. Important enough to hide them."

"And important enough for someone to kidnap Mom and Dad. These have to be what the kidnappers want, surely?"

"Most likely."

"And who do we know who is interested in ancient artifacts and treasure?" I said, tongue in cheek.

"The treasure hunters. Tamir and Omar," Jenna declared.

I was already heading for the door. "We need to go talk to them."

"Wait!" Remy grabbed my arm. "You can't go charging in. Remember, if it is them, they're dabbling in dark magic. And they're skilled enough to use it to hide your parents."

I hesitated. Darn it, she was right. "Let's go tell Blake. He can manipulate energy to create a shield. He could protect us if they tried anything."

"Wait," Remy said again, and I blew out an exasperated breath.

"Now what?"

"Aren't they at the caves? Didn't Nigel take them early this morning?"

"What's the time?" I asked no one in particular, grabbing my phone to check. Almost lunchtime. Andi had said she thought they'd be back early afternoon.

"Hold on," Jenna said, putting her fingers between the horizontal blind above the kitchen sink and peering out. "Nigel's truck is parked next to his trailer. If he's back, then the others should be back too."

Excellent. We were putting the journals away when it started. The screaming. Long, loud, and bloodcurdling.

My initial thought was that it was Gran. I knew she had the lung capacity to scream that loud. Slamming open the trailer door, I barreled outside and was three strides in, heading toward the swimming hole, when I realized the screams were coming from the other direction. Skidding to a halt, I glanced around in confusion.

Remy and Jenna joined me, with Jenna pointing towards the cabins. "Over there."

Blake staggered out of his cabin looking disheveled. I spared him a glance before jogging toward the cabin the screams were coming from. Bandit soon joined the cacophony of noise, barking. He must have moved like greased lightning to make it from the swimming hole to the cabin so quickly, and just as I wondered where Archie was, he came galloping around the side of the house.

"Oh my God, oh my God!" Kaylee came tumbling out of the cabin, tears smearing dark trails of mascara down her cheeks. Her hands were shaking as she pressed them to her chest as if struggling to breathe. Jenna reached her first.

"What is it? What's happened?" Jenna asked, wrapping an arm around Kaylee's shoulders. The girl trembled and shivered, her face reflecting pure terror as she pointed toward the open doorway.

"Harper, wait," Remy cautioned me, but I rushed to the door and stepped inside.

My stomach flip-flopped at the sight that greeted me, and I swallowed the bile rising in my throat. On the floor in a pool of blood was Tamir. Dead. Just to make sure, I crept closer and pressed two fingers against his neck. Although I was pretty sure the massive wound in his chest was a dead giveaway he was no longer alive, I'd hate to deprive the poor fellow of life-saving medical intervention on the assumption he was dead. My suspicions were confirmed. No pulse. His chest, complete with a gaping wound, was not moving. His eyes stared sightlessly at the ceiling.

I quickly rose and stood in the doorway. "Better call the police," I said to the others.

Kaylee wailed, and I nodded grimly. "It's Tamir. He's been murdered."

"Murdered?" Blake reached us. "Are you sure?"

Sucking my lips in and releasing them on a pop, I nodded. "Yup. Pretty sure. Check for yourself if you don't believe me."

His eyes zeroed in on the doorway behind me and he stepped around me to look inside. "Ah," he said grimly, "I see."

Andi was hurrying across the park toward us. "What is it? What's happened?"

Remy met her before she reached us and explained the situation.

"Oh, my!" Andi's hand reached for her throat. "And Kaylee? Is she okay?"

Kaylee was sobbing and hiccupping and Jenna led her over to her mother. "Why don't you take her up to the house and call the police?" she suggested. "We'll wait here."

"Yes, yes, I'll do that." Andi wrapped an arm around her daughter and led her back toward the house while the rest of us looked at each other, stunned.

"Where's Omar?" I asked, expecting to see the other treasure hunter after all the commotion. "And Nigel?"

"They're in the swimming hole," Gran said, making me jump.

"Geez. Where did you come from?" I gasped. I hadn't seen or heard her approach.

Gran shrugged. "Heard all the noise and came to investigate."

"Hold on," Blake said. "So you heard the screaming from down at the water hole and came to see what had happened, but Omar and Nigel stayed put?" Blake was right. It didn't make sense. The two men should have beaten Gran here.

"It's entirely possible they didn't hear. You're forgetting I have my witchy powers."

"Your witch powers don't include supersonic hearing, Gran," I pointed out, and she threw up her hands. "Okay fine! I heard nothing. I saw Bandit take off and figured something had caught his interest. I followed."

That sounded much more plausible.

"So, what's going on?" she asked, wrapping the towel that had been slung over her shoulders around her hips like a sarong.

"Someone has murdered Tamir," I said, stepping back so she could take a peek into the cabin.

"So they have." She nodded, then stepped further inside.

I stood in the doorway and watched her. "What are you doing? Be careful," I warned.

Ignoring me, Gran skirted around the pool of blood and stood at Tamir's head, eyes narrowing on his chest. "Well, this isn't good," she muttered.

"Of course it isn't." I rolled my eyes. A murder was never good.

"No. No." She shook her head and a droplet of water from her damp hair plopped onto Tamir's forehead. "Oops." She bent and wiped the water away with her thumb.

"Gran!" I hissed. "Don't contaminate the crime scene. Get out of there. Now."

"I'm coming, I'm coming." She joined us outside while we waited for the police.

***

"No press." Senior Sergeant Mick Gould stood with arms over his chest, refusing to budge.

"But—" Jenna protested, but he shook his head resolutely.

"All of you, go up to the house. I'll be up to take statements as soon as I'm done here."

Muttered grumbles met his words, but we obediently turned toward the house.

"Not you, Harper." Mick stopped me and I swiveled on my heel. "I'd like a word. In private," he added, when it looked like Blake would remain by my side. I nodded, gave Blake a nudge telling him it was okay. I wasn't in any danger and I was keen to hear what Mick had to say. Did he have any leads on my parents?

Blake nodded once, then spun on his heel and swiftly caught up with the others. Ignoring me, Mick stepped into the cabin and took photos with his phone. I stood in the doorway and watched, the coppery scent of blood filling my nostrils.

"You wanted a word?" I asked.

"I think you're involved." he said dispassionately, engrossed in snapping a picture of every inch of Tamir's cabin.

"What? How?" I spluttered. "I didn't do this!"

"I didn't say you did," Mick replied without looking at me. "I said you're involved. Too co-incidental that your parents disappeared from here, and now this? Somehow your family is involved, and I'd rather speak to you away from that circus." He nodded his head toward the big white house where everyone was waiting.

"I don't know how I can help," I said, stepping inside and keeping a wide berth around Tamir's body.

Mick busied himself with Tamir, crouching by his side and studying him intently. I turned my attention to what I'd missed before. The geospiral painted on the wall in Tamir's blood. I couldn't believe I hadn't seen it earlier, but maybe with the tangy scent of blood in the air, and the horror of his body on the floor at my feet, I could be forgiven for not noticing. It wasn't huge. About the size of my palm. Oh, it involved me all right. Whoever had my parents had done this. It was the only explanation. Glancing over my shoulder to check that Mick was distracted with the body, I quickly snapped a photo of the geospiral before sliding my phone back into my pocket, Mick none the wiser. I'd show it to Remy, see if she could figure out what it meant.

"Do you get a lot of murders in Arrowstrand?" I asked.

Mick glanced up at me. "Nope. This would be the first."

"Going to call in the big guns from Adelaide?"

"I'd like not to." Mick sighed, pushing aside Tamir's shirt with his pen. "But I may have to. This isn't looking good."

I snorted. "How could it possibly look worse?"

"I think someone has removed his heart."

I tried not to heave.

"I think there's something in there," Mick muttered. "It glinted when the light hit it."

Mick dug around in the case of equipment he'd brought with him, extracting a pair of tweezers. I screwed my eyes shut when he lowered them into Tamir's chest.

"What is that?" Mick asked more to himself than to me. My eyes popped open to see him holding something small and round in the tweezers. He grabbed a swab and wiped the blood from the object. It was a small round pebble just like the ones we'd found in my parents' trailer. And I'd bet it had a geospiral etched in its surface.

Mick dropped the stone into an evidence bag and sealed it. "The pattern looks the same as the one on the wall." Mick searched Tamir's pockets. When a gold pocket watch appeared, I gasped.

"What is it?" Mick picked up the pocket watch he'd placed on the floor and looked from it to me. "This watch look familiar?"

I nodded. "It's not actually a watch. It's a compass. And it belongs to my dad." My voice trembled, partly with shock, partly with anger.

Mick pressed on the button and the watch flipped open to reveal a compass. It had been in my family's possession for generations, handed down from son to son. Mick looked at me apologetically. "I will have to keep it as evidence for the time being." He slid it into another plastic evidence bag and sealed it.

My mind was a whirl. Had it been Tamir who'd broken into my parents' trailer and searched it? Had he taken them? But then, who had killed him? Were he and Omar in cahoots but had a falling out? But Gran had said Omar was down at the waterhole. But it was entirely possible he could have killed Tamir first, then gone to the waterhole, so he'd have an alibi.

Mick was scrolling through Tamir's phone when he paused and looked at me. "What?" I said warily.

Without a word he held the phone out so I could

see what was on the screen. A photo of my parents. Taken from a distance. I automatically reached for the phone, but Mick held it out of reach. "There are more," he said, dropping the phone into another evidence bag. "Looks like Tamir was spying on your folks."

"Do you think he took them?" My earlier euphoria at connecting with my mom fizzled and died. For Tamir was dead. He couldn't tell us where they were. And wherever he was holding them, it was somewhere no one would accidentally stumble across them. Although, now that Tamir was dead, whatever spell he'd cast would be broken, which meant I could easily connect to Mom and follow the trail to her location.

"He was certainly very interested in them. Have a look around, see if there's anything else belonging to your parents in this cabin. Here. Put these on." He tossed me a pair of gloves and I struggled to pull them over my sweaty skin. While I poked around in Tamir's cupboards and drawers looking for anything that may belong to my parents, Mick called for a coroner's van from a nearby town. Turned out Arrowstrand didn't have a morgue. Or hospital. They had a doctor travel in twice a week to run clinics and that was it.

After Mick was finished with the body, he draped a sheet over it, then turned his attention to me. "Find anything else?" I shook my head.

"You said in your report this morning that the caravan had been broken into?"

I nodded. "Whoever it was must have used a key," I said. "There were no signs of forced entry, but the place was a mess, like someone had rifled through everything, looking for something."

"But you noticed nothing was missing?"

I shook my head. "Not at the time. I mean, I didn't notice Dad's compass was missing because it could have easily been with him. So, it's hard to know what, if anything, is really missing."

Mick pondered my words for a minute, tapping his pen against his notebook where he'd been taking notes. "Okay. I want you to make a list of anything you *think* may be missing from your parents' van. It's too much of a coincidence that our victim not only had your father's compass but photos of your mom and dad on his phone too."

"You want me to do that now?" I snapped off the rubber gloves and held them out to him.

He took them and shoved them into his pocket. "Please. I will be here a while. I must wait for the coroner to arrive, and dust for prints. Then interview everyone up at the house. So, if you can get that list sorted and I'll meet you up there when I can? Oh, and can you ask them not to leave? I need to get their statements."

"Will do." Stepping outside into the bright afternoon sunshine, I saw Bandit and Archie sitting side by side, silently waiting. As if sensing my mood, they quietly followed me to the trailer, electing to wait outside under the shade of the canopy while I went through my parents' belongings—again—to see if anything was missing. The trouble was...how would I know?

EIGHT

I found it shoved inside a sock, of all things. A velvet jewelers' box. Mom wasn't much into jewelry, so I was curious what the box could contain. A ring was my best guess, going on the size of the box. Flipping open the lid, I frowned. Instead of a ring, I found nothing. Why would Mom hide an empty box? I sat on the end of the bed and turned the box over and over in my hand. I doubted Mom would be wearing the ring now. She would save it for special occasions, when she got dressed up. So where was it? It must have been special for her to hide it, but shoving it in a sock in the back of a drawer wasn't the safest of locations, so I figured it had more sentimental value than monetary.

The box slipped from my fingers, hitting the floor.

The block of foam fell out, revealing a folded piece of paper tucked in the box's bottom.

Quickly unfolding the note, I scanned the words written there in my dad's handwriting. A love note from Dad to Mom, telling her that the alexandrite gemstone in the setting was as precious as his love for her.

Ah, it made more sense now. Dad had given Mom the gemstone ring for their anniversary. I'd have to research just how valuable an alexandrite gemstone is, because it was definitely missing and considering my mom doesn't even wear her wedding ring, I doubted she was wearing the ring now. Tucking the note back into the ring box, I snapped it closed. I'd give it to Mick when he took my statement, but I'd also ask Jenna, with her investigative skills, to see if she could trace where Dad had bought it.

Before I left the trailer, I had one more thing to do. Tamir was dead, meaning the spell hiding my parents was broken. I could end this here and now astral-walking.

Sitting cross-legged on the bed, I focused my energy, closed my eyes and prepared for the whooshing sensation of traveling down the magical power lines like a roller coaster on steroids. Only instead of the heart-pounding, nausea-inducing ride, I got nothing. Zip. My eyes snapped open and my brows furrowed. That was not the result I'd been expecting! Tamir was dead, it should break the spell.

Unless he hadn't cast the spell. Disappointment weighed heavy on my shoulders as I made my way up to the house, pausing to watch a white van pull up next to Mick's police vehicle. Here to collect the body I assumed.

Hearing voices from the rear of the house, I took the side staircase to the deck out back where the others had gathered. Omar and Nigel had come up from the swimming hole and were sitting with Kaylee, who was no longer crying, although her eye makeup was a total mess. Omar kept patting her knee while Nigel sat back with his arms crossed over his chest, a blank expression on his face. Jenna, Gran, Remy and Blake sat at a wooden table further down the deck.

Jenna saw me first and jumped up. "There you are! What's going on? Why did he let you stay and send the rest of us up here?"

"He thinks this involves my parents." I told them about the compass we'd found in Tamir's pocket and, lowering my voice to a whisper, I filled them in on the geospiral pebble found in his chest and the one painted on the wall in his blood.

Remy was frowning. "This doesn't sound good," she muttered darkly.

"Anything using blood magic isn't good," Gran

said, uncharacteristically subdued. "What else, Harper?"

Gran could see right through me; she'd always been able to. "I thought Tamir must have cast the spell to hide my parents, so I figured with him dead, it would break the spell. So, I tried to astral-walk, only I got nothing. A big fat zero like before."

"So Tamir wasn't behind the spell," Jenna whispered, whipping out her phone and madly typing in notes.

Blake eyed me. "Tamir could hardly have cast the spell and then killed himself," he pointed out.

"Yes, well." I cleared my throat. "I figured it was worth a shot. But Tamir was involved somehow. He had Dad's compass. And photos of them on his phone."

"The question is why?" Jenna asked.

Remy was tapping her chin with her finger. "Tamir and Omar are treasure hunters, so we have to assume they're here for the copper pyramid. Most people think it's in the ABC range. Only your parents figured it out, Harper. It's here. Has to be."

"So what? Tamir and Omar followed them here?" My eyes zeroed in on Omar who had given up on consoling Kaylee and was now sitting back dragging on a cigarette. "And what about him?" I nodded in Omar's direction. "Did he find the scroll and then kill Tamir so he wouldn't have to share?"

"Sloppy of him if he did," Blake said. "If it were me, I would have taken the compass, and either deleted those photos off the phone or got rid of the phone altogether."

"Sorry to keep you waiting." Mick appeared at the top of the stairs, his face grim. "I will take a brief statement from each of you and then I'll need you to come into the station tomorrow to be fingerprinted."

"What?" Nigel grumbled, not looking happy at this turn of events.

"To rule you out as suspects," Mick added.

"Oh yes, of course, that makes sense." Andi nodded, cradling Joey in her arms.

Mick's eyes zeroed in on Kaylee. "I'll start with you, Kaylee. Tell me what happened."

Kaylee's hands shook, but her voice was calm as she said, "I'd gone to Tamir's cabin to clean it. I knocked on the door. When there was no answer, I assumed he was still at the caves, so I used the master key to unlock the door and get the cleaning done while he was out. That's when I discovered his body."

"Do you normally clean the cabins at midday?" Mick asked, glancing up from his notes.

Kaylee shrugged. "I do them when I can get to them. I worked at the hotel last night, so I slept in this morning."

Mick nodded. "And you?" He nodded at Omar. "What's your name?"

"You know who I am," Omar drawled, dragging on his cigarette.

"For the record." Mick eyeballed him and Omar crushed out his cigarette in the ashtray in front of him, exhaling a plume of smoke he said, "Omar Ali."

"And your relationship with the deceased?"

"Tamir and I were partners. Here on business."

"What sort of business?"

"Relics and artifacts."

"So, treasure hunters then." Mick scribbled in his notepad.

Omar grinned. "That is what some people call us, yes."

"And you're here from?"

"Croatia. We arrived last week."

"To see the caves?"

"Exactly. There are rumors about a copper scroll being hidden in the Arrowstrand Caves. We decided to check it out for ourselves."

Remy and I exchanged a look. So, they knew about the scroll.

"And where were you this morning?"

"Tamir and I went to the caves early. Dawn. Nigel took us. We came back just before lunch. Tamir was tired—said he didn't get much sleep last night, so he wanted a nap. I thought I'd spend a couple of hours at the water hole. Nigel joined me since he didn't have a tour this afternoon."

I opened my mouth to argue that Nigel could have taken us to the caves if he'd let us know he was free, but Blake nudged me to keep my mouth shut. I snapped it closed.

"Nigel." Mick turned his attention to the guide. "You corroborate Omar's story?"

"Yep." Nigel nodded. "Took the two of them to the caves, came back around noon thereabouts. When Omar suggested a dip I figured why not? Was down there when this whole hullabaloo started. The old chick can vouch for us. She was there."

"Hey!" Gran snapped her fingers. "Who you be calling old chick?"

"Gran," I warned, placing my hand on her arm. "Let the sergeant do his job."

Mick smiled briefly, turning his attention to Gran. "You were at the water hole too, ma'am?"

"Sure was, soaking up the Australian sun. These two turned up, but not together."

Mick raised an eyebrow. "Oh?" he prompted.

"The old skinny twig arrived first. Couldn't tell you what the time was. Around midday I guess, but it was a good ten minutes if not longer before Omar turned up."

"Thank you." Mick nodded, not giving anything away. He glanced at Blake. "And you?"

"I was in my cabin. Taking a nap," Blake said.

"Another tired one, eh?" Mick muttered. "And were you... alone?"

"Yes, I was alone. I was helping Harper this morning and then I wasn't feeling so good so went to lie down for a while."

"And what were you helping Harper with?"

"I don't think that's relevant." Blake stonewalled and Mick looked at him with narrowed eyes.

"That's right. You're a lawyer."

"Interesting that you already knew that," Blake shot back, and I looked from one to the other in surprise. Good point. Jenna's fingers were moving like wildfire across the screen of her phone as she typed up her own notes.

"Harper? Was Mr. Tennant with you earlier?" Mick asked.

"Yes, he was. We were trying to work out what had happened to my parents."

"I see. And what did you discover?"

"Not much," I lied.

There was a pause then Mick continued, "And what time did Mr. Tennant leave your caravan?"

I shrugged. "Mid-morning, I guess. I didn't notice the time."

"And then what did you do?"

"Jenna and Remy joined me and we spent the rest of the morning going through my parents' journals to see if we could find any clues to their disappearance."

"Playing amateur detective?"

Gran snorted. "You have no idea. My granddaughter solved two murders in Whitefall Cove. I'd hardly call her amateur."

"Gran. Shush."

Mick looked at us for a moment before shrugging and turning his attention to Andi. "And you?"

"I've been in the house all morning doing laundry and looking after this little guy." She nodded at the sleeping bundle in her arms.

He nodded, jotted down something in his notebook, then closed it and slid it into the breast pocket of his shirt. "I'm going to have to ask that none of you leave town. And if you think of anything else, remember anything, please let me know." He glanced around again, frowning. "Where's Colin?"

"He had sunrise and sunset tours in Darana so he stayed overnight. I'm not expecting him home until tomorrow."

Mick raised his eyebrows. "He stays overnight? Darana is only an hour's drive away."

"He says it's too risky to drive after a tour when he's tired. Roos on the road and all," she said defensively, and I looked at her more closely. Her cheeks were flushed, and her eyes flashed. I cocked my head, thinking. An hour wasn't that much of a commute to a job. Hardly an excuse to not come home when your day was done. Andi twisted her wedding ring around and around on her finger and my eyes followed the movement. Something was up in the Webb's marriage. There was more behind Colin spending the night away. Maybe they were fighting. Or he was a snorer. Or she was. There were a multitude of reasons why he hadn't come home, but my mind, full of Simon's cheating betrayal, immediately zeroed in on the possibility that Colin was cheating on his wife. My heart went out to her and before I even realized I was moving, I'd crossed to her side and wrapped an arm around her shoulders in solidarity. She gave me a small, grateful smile.

By the time Mick left, the sun was low on the horizon. Omar had left as soon as Mick did. Nigel slung an arm around Andi's shoulders and gave her a squeeze before he too departed. Kaylee couldn't get inside fast enough and we all heard her bedroom door slam. Poor girl, it must have been traumatic to find Tamir's body like that.

"I'd better go check on her," Andi whispered, tears in her eyes. We left as quietly as we could, automatically wandering toward my trailer where Bandit and Archie were stretched out under the awning dozing.

"What next?" I asked no one in particular.

"I say we get cleaned up and head into town for dinner. I'm starving. I totally missed lunch. Then we can regroup," Jenna said.

"Good idea," Blake agreed, swiveling on his heel and striding toward his cabin.

"Meet at mine in twenty minutes!" Remy called after him. He raised his hand showing he'd heard her but didn't turn around.

"Is it just me or is he acting weird?" Jenna asked.

"It's not just you. He's been out of sorts ever since he helped me astral-walk this morning," I replied, watching as Blake's long strides ate up the dirt in no time.

"I'm going to take a shower," Gran announced. "We're meeting at yours in twenty, right?" she said to Remy, having no interest in gossiping about Blake and his weird behavior.

"Affirmative."

Calling Archie inside, I dished up his food and sat on the bed, watching him scarf it down without barfing, when I suddenly remembered I hadn't told Mick about the jewelry box and the missing ring. Presumed missing ring. I'd give it to him tomorrow when I signed my statement and gave my fingerprints.

With a sigh, I picked up the remote and switched on the TV, watching a mindless game show until it was time to leave.

Dressed in a full-length, figure-hugging, sequin-covered evening dress of canary yellow, Gran locked her cabin door and pulled up her skirt, revealing rainbow-colored converses, and made her way to Remy's Land Rover.

"What are you wearing?" I snorted, blinking from the dazzling glare of her dress.

"I dressed for dinner." Gran huffed, heaving herself up onto the seat next to me. "You should do the same sometime. Maybe if you dressed in something a little more revealing, you'd get more action with Blake. Can't help but notice things have stalled there."

"Gran!" I protested, feeling heat creep up my neck and into my face. The fact that she was right compounded my embarrassment. As per usual. Despite the almost kiss the other night, Blake had made no moves to progress our relationship—if it even was one.

"What's up?" Jenna asked, joining us. "You been friend zoned?" she asked.

"No." I grumbled, but there wasn't much conviction in it. Maybe I had, and I hadn't noticed. Back in Whitefall Cove Blake had been flirty, and darkly moody at the same time. Here he was... I didn't know how to describe it. And ever since helping me astral-walk he was decidedly off. I'd put it down to the fact the super highway sensation of astral-walking turns your stomach inside out and I hadn't warned him. Maybe he was suffering motion sickness. It sounded lame, even to my own ears.

Remy came bursting out of her cabin. "Harper! Can I leave Bandit in your van again?"

"Oh sure. Here's the key." I was already strapped in the car but the door stood open so I held the key out and she dashed past, scooping it out of my palm as she jogged across the trailer park to my trailer on the other side, Bandit happily bounding along by her side.

Gran, seated between Jenna and myself, grabbed each of our hands. "It will be a blood moon in two nights."

I nodded. "Correct. And Kaylee's twenty-first."

"I fear today was just the beginning," she continued on, ignoring my reference to Kaylee's upcoming birthday. "I want you two to protect yourselves. No good will come from this."

"It does seem ominous," I agreed. "That reminds me, Gran, I need to ask you something. Dad gave Mom an alexandrite gemstone ring for their anniversary. Do you know anything about it? When he gave it to her? Does she wear it?"

Gran snorted. "Your father should have saved his money. Your mother doesn't wear jewelry. Not even her wedding ring."

"I know, but I was wondering if she wore it as a necklace or something?"

"Have you ever seen your mother wear necklaces? Or bracelets? Or earrings? Nope. Why?"

"Because it's missing. I found an empty ring box."

"How do you know what was inside if it was empty?" Jenna asked. I told her about the note.

Remy returned and climbed behind the wheel. "Ready?"

"What about Blake?" I asked, looking over to his cabin where the door remained closed.

"He's not coming," Remy said, slamming her door and gunning the engine. "He wasn't feeling well, doesn't want to pass it around to you guys. He's hoping to sleep it off."

"Oh." I swallowed the hurt that Blake had turned to Remy instead of me.

Remy glanced at me over her shoulder. "Anyone want to ride up front?"

"I will!" Gran shouted, elbowing me madly to get out of her way.

"Okay, okay. Hang on." Dodging her elbows, I unfastened my belt and hopped out, helping Gran down, then climbing back in, watching in resignation when Gran hiked her evening dress so high you could practically see her underwear—I sincerely hoped she was wearing underwear, it wasn't always a given with my gran. Once everyone was strapped in and the doors closed, we were off.

"Remy, what do you know about the gemstone alexandrite?" Jenna asked, head buried in her phone once again.

"Oh, alexandrite is beautiful. And not very common. It's made up of a rare combination of minerals that includes titanium, iron and chromium, giving it color-changing abilities. Why's that?"

"Harper's mom had a ring with an alexandrite gemstone in it and now it's missing. So, it's valuable?"

"Well yes, it's valuable. But we're not talking diamonds here though," Remy said. "Remind me when we get back and I'll look into it. I'm not sure alexandrite is used in jewelry that much."

As soon as we stepped into the front bar of the hotel, my stomach grumbled. Loudly. I laughed self-consciously and pressed my hand to my protesting stomach. Jenna wasn't the only one who'd missed lunch.

Jenna headed to the bar for menus while the rest of us settled at a table by the window. Petrina gave us a wave. Given today's events I assumed Kaylee wouldn't be working tonight.

"Gran, what you said earlier about the blood moon..." It had been bothering me the entire car ride in. "What do you think it all means? And how do we protect ourselves?"

"I'll make some charms tonight. Wear them at all times," Gran said, nodding sagely.

"What's this about the blood moon? What did I miss?" Remy looked at our faces, one brow arched.

"It's a blood moon in two nights. Coupled with the dead bird, Gran thinks it's a sign."

"Well, you can't ignore the fact that we also have a dead body," Jenna added.

"And the geospirals," I said.

Remy visibly paled. Slowly she leaned back in her chair and stared at me with dazed eyes. "What?" I whispered, reaching for her hand. "What is it?"

"It can't be," she muttered, shaking her head.

"What can't it be?" Jenna prodded.

Blinking, Remy sat forward. "The blood sacrifice and dark magic and geospirals and alexandrite gemstone"—she ticked them off on her fingers—"are all part of a ritual."

"I knew it," Gran grumbled, "I knew something bad was coming. I can feel it."

"You're not wrong," Remy told her. "I need to get back, look this up." She rose to her feet, but Jenna clasped her wrist, forcing her back down.

"Hold on, hold on. Let's eat first, okay? Then we'll go. You can't work on an empty stomach."

"Jenna's right. Let's order dinner. We won't linger, just eat and then go. Sorry, Gran," I added, knowing Gran had been looking forward to hustling more men at the pool table.

"Not a problem with me, love. We've got those charms to make as well."

We quickly ordered our meals, our thoughts consumed with Remy's revelation, all eager to head back to find out what it all meant. But first—food.

<hr>

"Harper. Was Tamir's heart missing by any chance?" We were back in Remy's cabin amongst old leather-bound books and her industrial plated laptop. Gran was burning incense and muttering an incantation so we wouldn't be overheard. Archie and Bandit lay curled together on Remy's bed, their soft snores bouncing off the walls in the bout of silence that followed Remy's question.

I cleared my throat. "Mick seemed to think so. I didn't look. I'm guessing that's pertinent?"

"I think whoever is behind this is calling forth the Goddess who will bring immortality and great riches."

"Does this Goddess have a name?" Jenna asked.

Remy shook her head, turning the pages on the book spread out before her. "That's the weird part. No." The air was heavy with the scent of incense and the wind outside buffeted the cabin in a sudden gust. Goosebumps broke out over my skin, along with an impending sense of doom.

"Tell us about the spell," I croaked, but I already knew, deep down inside it wasn't good. It was bad. Hell bad.

Remy cleared her throat. "It's kinda gross," she warned. I'd figured as much and motioned for her to continue. Gran paused to listen.

"The ceremony is conducted in three parts. The first two are the nights leading up to the blood moon. The third is the night of the blood moon." The wind howled again, and the cabin shook, as if the elements themselves were trying to silence Remy's words.

"Part one is done, isn't it?" It wasn't a question. More of a statement of fact. Tamir had been the first sacrifice. They had cut his heart from his chest and replaced it with a geospiral rock. Remy inclined her head.

"Sacrifice one," she read from the book. "A human

male heart is removed from the body and burned. In its place, the symbol of the Goddess."

"A glyph rock. Is that the same as the geospiral ones?" Jenna asked.

Remy nodded. "A geospiral is a form of glyph. And as your parents discovered, Harper, they are a language. The circles mean different things. We just need to decode them."

"So, what's next on this crazy ass agenda?" Gran demanded.

"Sacrifice two," Remy continued. "A human female heart is removed from the body and burned. In its place, the symbol of the Goddess."

Chills danced up my spine, a sense of foreboding so deep my bones ached with it. A woman would die tonight. Gran's eyes were shrewd as she looked at each of us around the table. "It will not be one of us. I won't allow it."

"To be safe, I think we should stay together." Jenna sounded confident, but I could see the slight tremor in her hands. She was as freaked out and scared as the rest of us. I wished Blake were here, a strong alpha male presence would have calmed our nerves, but he hadn't answered his door when I'd dropped by after dinner. He was either a very deep sleeper, or he wasn't there.

"And tomorrow night? The culmination of all this, assuming whoever is behind this is successful in finding a female victim tonight?" I asked.

"Sacrifice three." Remy looked right at me and my heart stopped beating. "Two sacrifices. Hearts in love. A male *and* female."

Gran gasped, a rattling wheeze. I'd never heard such a noise from her before and I touched her arm in concern. "You okay?" I whispered.

"They have Judith and Keith. Saving them for the final sacrifice," Gran said, voice shaking with anger. "For the ritual to work the two hearts have to be filled with love—for each other. I'd say there's not a lot of that around these parts, slim pickings. So, when word got out that they were heading back to Whitefall Cove, the killer made their move. Took them to use later."

"Oh God. You're right. That makes perfect sense." Laying my arms on the table I briefly rested my head on them. "And the dead bird, and missing ring, they're all part of the overall ceremony, right?"

"Yes," Remy said.

Gran nudged me. "Okay, buck up, kiddo, we've got work to do. First up, let's finish these protection charms. Then you need to do what you do best."

I sat up. "What's that?"

"Find out who the killer is. Focus on the clues. Someone killed Tamir. You just need to find out who, before tomorrow night. You need a murder board."

She was right. Rather than focusing on the horror

of the dark magic, focus on the clues. Whoever did this was human. And they were here, under our very noses.

"Remy, you have any Post-it notes in your stash?" I asked, standing up.

She nodded. "Sure. Here, catch." She tossed me a square, yellow pack of Post-it notes. Jenna was digging around in her bag and produced a marker, holding it out.

"Okay ladies." I smiled, pushing down the fear and worry. "Let's do this. Who do we have?"

"Omar Ali." Jenna was reading from the notes on her phone. I wrote Omar's name down on a Post-it and stuck it to the wall. "He had a ten-minute gap between when they came back from the caves to when he appeared at the swimming hole."

"And the bean-pole guide. What's his face," Gran said.

"Nigel Franic," Jenna supplied. "He had a smaller window of opportunity when he separated from Omar and Tamir to get changed into swimmers."

"Cutting out a heart would take time," Remy pointed out.

I tapped the marker against my palm. "It didn't look that surgical," I admitted. "It was...rough. A lot of blood."

"And you'd have to get through the chest bone. So, you'd need to be strong," Jenna said.

"So, we're thinking a man?" Remy said.

"But you can't discount the possibility that more than one person is involved," I pointed out. "Omar and Nigel could have been working together. Who else do we have?"

"The Webbs. Andi, Kaylee, and the mysterious Colin," Jenna read from her phone. "Maybe Colin is ducking back with no one noticing, doing the deed and hightailing it out of here all without being seen."

"It's possible."

"What about Andi and Kaylee? I mean Andi seems as sweet as pie. I couldn't imagine her hurting a fly, let alone cutting a man's heart out of his chest," I said.

"Kaylee has a lot of angst and anger. I heard her arguing with her mom, but that's not unusual for someone her age," Gran said.

I added all the names to the wall.

"We need to interview them. Motives and alibis."

"But we need to be subtle about it," I pointed out. "We can't tip our hand that we know what's going on."

"Play dumb, you mean?" Jenna's lips twisted in a grimace.

"Yes. We can't just go marching up to them demanding answers."

"Harper's right." Remy closed her laptop. "We have to be smart about this. We're going to the caves with Nigel in the morning. That seems a good place to start."

TEN

"You look different this morning, Blake." Remy cocked her head and studied him. I followed suit. She was right. His hair was more styled, he'd wound a scarf around his neck and his T-shirt was tucked in.

"Thanks. I'm trying something different. You like?" He gave a little twirl and my eyebrows shot up into my hairline. Had he turned gay overnight? Remy laughed, then quickly sobered when he shot her a cold as steel frown.

"You look great," she assured him. "You even shaved."

He ran his hands over his smooth cheeks. "Wanna feel?" he asked her, but she shook her head.

"Nope. I'm good thanks."

Clearing my throat, I drew everyone's attention.

"Are we all ready? Gran? Are you sure you won't come? I don't like leaving you here by yourself."

We'd survived the night in Remy's cabin, alive and intact. Andi and Kaylee were accounted for, so I allowed myself to relax, just a notch. The killer hadn't progressed to the second stage of their evil plan, which meant I was one step closer to finding Mom and Dad. Today's plan was to search the caves.

"I'll be fine, love." Gran was already dressed in her bikini, a large red brimmed hat shielding her face. "And I've got Archie and Bandit to keep me safe. I intend to spend the morning by the waterhole—less chance of anyone trying anything nefarious out in the open like that."

"Wear your charm," I warned her, my fingers going to my charm tied around my wrist.

"Already am." She wriggled her foot, drawing my attention to the woven cord encircling her ankle. "Don't worry about me, you focus on finding Judith and Keith."

"Morning folks!" Nigel appeared, the heavy scent of tobacco clinging to him. "How many do we have today?"

"Just us," I said. "Gran won't be joining us."

"Okey dokey. So, you can ride with me or bring your own vehicle, the choice is yours. However, if you ride with me, be warned I can only stay a couple of hours. This is meant to be my day off and I've got errands to run today."

"You're working on your day off?" Jenna asked.

Nigel shrugged. "To make up for the mix-up yesterday. It's all good, don't worry about it."

"We'll take my vehicle," Remy interrupted. "That way we can stay as long as we want without disrupting your plans."

"Load up and follow me." Nigel was chirpy this morning, and my eyes met Jenna's as we headed toward Remy's Land Rover. Nigel struck me as the quieter type, broody, maybe tired and fed up with dealing with tourists and counting down the days until retirement. Of course, that was just my impression, I had no idea if I was right or not.

The track to the caves was rough, windy, but so worth it. We eventually cleared the rock-hewn dried-out creek beds to find ourselves in a clearing that Mother Nature had created. Instead of dirt, the clearing was one massive slab of rock. Nigel's four wheel drive was parked on the opposite side and Remy pulled up next to him, killing the engine.

She swiveled to look at us. "I will focus on mapping this place, and doing stuff for work, so I'll leave it to you to ask the important questions of our intrepid guide."

"Got it." Climbing out, I grabbed my backpack

from the floor and slipped it over my shoulders. Jenna and Blake did the same, while Remy opened the rear of the Land Rover and pulled out a larger duffle. Digging around in it, she pulled out a square box, clipped it to her belt, then slipped a head-mounted flashlight on. Another piece of equipment joined the first on her belt.

"What's all that?" Nigel asked, curiosity drawing him closer.

Remy didn't look up. "I work in ancient artifacts," she explained. "These are tools to help me determine if an artifact is the real deal or fake."

"You're expecting to find artifacts down here?" Nigel scoffed. "Fat chance of that."

Remy winked at me but remained silent and the penny dropped. Her equipment wasn't to identify artifacts at all. I'd ask her about it once Nigel was out of earshot.

He began handing out glossy printed maps to each of us. They were very basic.

"Gather round," he said, holding a map aloft. It fluttered in the breeze. "Obviously we're here because you want to see for yourselves where the Joneses were exploring." His voice was even, no inflection of emotion. "They were experienced spelunkers—cave explorers—so I wasn't with them most of the time. Omar and Tamir kept me busy, as the pair of them apparently have no sense of direction." The last was uttered with a small shake of his head. "Anyway. This"

—he pointed to a spot on his map—"is where they were last. So that's where we'll start today. Has anyone done this before?"

"I have," Remy said. "Many times."

"Excellent. You're now the team leader." Nigel dug a hand in the pocket of his shorts and pulled out a glow stick. "I'll be marking the trail with these, so you can find your way out. Like I said, I'll be taking you through the cave system up to this point, but I can't stay. These are your exit. They will stay alight for twenty-four hours so you have plenty of time, all I ask is that you pick them up on your way out, so we aren't littering the caves with burned out glow sticks."

Remy nodded, folding her arms over her chest as she listened to Nigel's instructions.

"As you can imagine, it's dark in there. There are no lights. You have your torches and glow sticks. Stick close together. Now if you'll follow me into the entry cave, I want to show you something."

We obediently followed him into the first cavern, which was massive. Easily the size of a football field. The entrance was the size of a tennis court; we could have driven our vehicles inside. But the pièce de résistance was the hole in the roof, a circle, letting a stream of light in. Beneath that light was a small hill covered in green grass with a tree growing on top. The tree was fully grown and still didn't reach the roof of the cavern. We traipsed across the floor of the cavern until we reached the mirage, which was stunning, beautiful in its dark surroundings.

"Nature can do wonderful things," Nigel said, pride in his voice. "You'll find a couple of these air holes throughout the caves, giving a reprieve from the darkness." He held up his map again and pointed to two different areas. "Here and here."

"How long will it take us to get to the area my parents were exploring?" I asked.

"An hour, maybe less depending on how fast we travel," he answered. "Hope you're not claustrophobic. Some tunnels are narrow. You can stand, but you'll have to shuffle through sideways. Other parts are low, and you'll have to crawl. Pleased to see you're all wearing long pants. Sensible."

"Remy warned us," Jenna said in acknowledgement to our spelunking expert friend.

"Okay, let's go. Stick together, don't lag behind. If you want to stop, we all stop. Do not get separated from the group."

Nigel led the way, Jenna directly behind, then me, Blake, and finally Remy.

Jenna struck up a conversation with Nigel, chatting away about the differences between Australia and America as we made our way through the main cavern and into one of three tunnels. Torch in one hand and map in the other, I followed, half listening to their conversation. Behind me Remy turned on one of her gadgets and a light flashed as it flared to life. "What is that?" I whispered.

"Energy detector," she whispered back. "It'll alert me of any other living creatures within our vicinity."

I crossed my fingers it would find Mom and Dad, although as we were plunged into complete darkness except for the beams of our torches I shuddered at the thought of being kept down here for days, for surely their batteries would have died by now, along with any glow sticks. Although, I argued silently in my head, it depended on how many glow sticks you had with you. They were explorers, therefore well equipped. And if one glow-stick lasted twenty-four hours, they'd have only used four, and from memory, my dad always had his pockets stuffed with the things whenever they were on an expedition. Ditto food and water. They'd have enough for a few days. I found that comforting.

"Have you always run the tours Nigel?" Jenna asked.

"Yep. Colin takes care of the four-wheel-drive stuff, I do underground. I know these caves like the back of my hand, used to come here just for fun when Arrowstrand was a sheep farm."

"So, this was your R and R?"

"Absolutely."

"But didn't you say part of the caves were unexplored? Because they're so vast?"

"They're a labyrinth, all right. I meant, the caves and tunnels we're passing through now I know like the back of my hand. I've been visiting for years, which is why it made perfect sense for me to run tours of these parts of the caves."

"What about to the north?" Remy asked, "It looks like it ends abruptly on the map."

"There was a cave in," he explained. "So we keep the tours contained to this area. And it's where your parents were focusing their efforts," he added for my benefit.

"And did they find any indications that there's a copper pyramid down here?" I asked.

Nigel laughed and I could just make out the silhouette of him shaking his head. "Nope, not that I know of. Omar and Tamir were convinced it existed too."

"Oh?" Remy prodded.

"Seems they were following the same leads as the Joneses. Or plain out following the Joneses and hoping to pip them at the post," he said. "Keith and Judith had a theory that the circular etchings found at Chambers Gorge and Sacred Canyon form a map. Pointing here. I've looked at it a million times and I can't see it." He shrugged. "But I know Australia sits on the 44th Parallel ley line and nothing can be ruled out."

"You know about Grid Point 44?" Remy asked, surprise in her tone.

"Yup," Nigel replied. "Careful now, watch your heads, we're branching off here."

I duly noted on my map our location and lowered my head as we shuffled through a tunnel. It was as black as Hades down here and the further inward we traveled, the colder we got. Jenna had lapsed into silence and the only sound was that of our footfalls scuffing over the dirt and rocks. It smelled different too. Earthy and musky. There was a cracking sound, a flare of light, and Nigel dropped another glow stick when one tunnel intersected another. It was comforting that even without Nigel we'd be able to find our way out, for despite following on my map I had a feeling I'd never be able to make it out on my own.

Although we had the backup of Remy. I could hear her scribbling something into the notebook she had resting on the energy-reading device. I wasn't sure if she was writing directions or just notes on the cave structure or things she observed. To me this was all dark rock of little interest, but to someone like Remy it must be a treasure trove of delight. After what felt like hours we finally arrived at our destination. Another cave with its own built-in skylight.

"Here we are, folks. This—as far as I know—is where the Joneses concentrated their efforts." Nigel stood, hands on hips, and peered around in the dim light. We still needed torches, but the light peeking through the small hole above us was enough to lift the pitch-black darkness.

"Really?" The trace of skepticism in Remy's voice had my head snapping in her direction. I trusted her judgement over Nigel's.

"Like I said, as far as I know." Nigel shrugged, unconcerned whether or not Remy believed him. As far as he was concerned, he'd done his job. He gave a talk on the origins of the caves, how inland Australia was once an ocean, and where we were standing was once underwater. He talked of stalactites and stalagmites and then bid us farewell, reminding us to follow the glow sticks out, and to pick them up as we did so.

"What do you think?" I asked Remy, who was studying an area of the rock wall.

"I call bullshit," she said, not bothering to look up. "I don't know if he is lying intentionally, or if this is where he believes your parents were working, but I can say for a fact they were not working here."

"Oh?"

"Look around." She straightened and indicated the cave. "What do you see?"

"A cave?" I said tentatively.

She grinned. "And what else? Beyond rocks and dirt." She paused, waiting while I looked. Honestly? I didn't see what she was seeing.

"It's what's missing," she finally said. "Your

parents' gear. If they were excavating fossils and rocks and things, their gear would be here. They wouldn't cart it in and out. They treated this like a normal expedition, meaning they'd have a crate of tools with them, lamps, supplies. None of that is here."

"Maybe they took it back to camp? When they knew they were coming home, they would have packed up?" I pointed out.

"But they didn't know." Remy jumped on it. "You called them in the middle of the night, right? They jumped online, booked tickets, packed up and hit the road, heading to Adelaide ready to take that flight home. They wouldn't have come down to the caves to collect their gear. That would have taken up hours of valuable time. They fully intended to come back and continue on with this expedition once they sorted their business back home."

Jenna joined us. "So, you're saying either they were here, and someone has taken their gear, or this isn't the area they were working."

"I'm saying this isn't the area they were working. This is one of Nigel's typical tour destinations because of the skylight. It's been trampled through dozens of times, picked at, photographed to death. There are no archeological surprises here."

"He lied," I said grimly. "So, we're no closer to finding my parents."

"Not necessarily. This gadget, the one that

searches for energy signatures, I can try to track them through this. If they were off the beaten path, so to speak, there could be remnants of their energy left behind, enough for me to pick up."

Jenna was nodding. "And it probably won't work here—not for what we want—because this is a heavily populated area!"

Remy was nodding. "Exactly! I think Nigel led us away from where your parents were working."

"Why would he do that?" I mused. "Do you think he has them?"

Remy shrugged. "It could be something more mundane. Did you notice how chummy he is with Omar? Maybe Omar slipped him some dollars to lead us away, giving him time to find the scroll."

"What do you think?" I asked Blake, who was touching the cave wall a few feet away. "You're the lawyer with razor sharp instincts. Was Nigel lying?"

"Hmmm?" Blake didn't turn from his inspection of the rock face. "Have you seen this?" he asked, ignoring my question altogether. "It's so pretty. And wonderfully amazing." Remy shone a torch on what he was looking at. A fossil of what appeared to be a combination of a butterfly with a fish. It could have been either.

"Not helping, Tennant," Remy muttered. To me and Jenna she said, "I say we head in the other direction."

"Towards the cave-in?" Jenna said.

"But was there really a cave-in? Or was that another ruse to throw us off the scent, to keep us away from that particular area?"

"I promise I won't lead us into a cave-in. We'll head in that general direction, if I pick up any energy signatures, we'll follow it."

"It could be picking up Omar and Tamir though," I pointed out.

"Uh yeah, who were clearly following your parents around," Jenna replied. "I'm with Remy. Let's go."

We were across the cave and heading out the tunnel when I realized Blake was still at the rock wall oohing and ahhing over the fossil. Seriously?

"Blake!" I called, annoyance tinging my voice. "Come on."

He glanced up in surprise. "Oh? We're going? Okay. Bye-bye butterfly." And he pressed a kiss to his fingers and pressed them against the fossil. Oh, my good lord, what was wrong with him?

CHAPTER
ELEVEN

"Hold up!" Remy raised her fist in the air, and we all staggered to a halt behind her. "This isn't right," she muttered. We were at an intersection of tunnels and a glow stick lay on the ground showing we should go left.

"What's up?" Moving to stand by her side, I looked left, then right. Both tunnels looked the same. I studied the map Nigel had given me.

Remy snatched it from my hand and turned it over before giving it back. "You're looking at it upside down," she said by way of explanation. "And that map is useless," she added, voice filled with disdain. "It doesn't show half of the detail. It's a glossy keepsake for tourists, nothing more."

"So, what do we do then?"

"I've been using this to map as we go." She tapped the other gadget attached to her belt. "It reads the land formations around us and has been creating a 3D map ever since we entered the caves. Between that and my own sense of direction, *that* is not the exit." She pointed to the left, then let her arm drop. "Someone moved the glow stick."

"Say what now?" Jenna shone her torch on the ground where the glow stick lay, then to the opposite side where it should have been. There were scuffed footprints but nothing discernable. Did Nigel move the glow stick? Or was someone else down here? Someone like Omar, who would do anything to stop us from finding the scroll. Little did he know I couldn't give a damn about the scroll. All I wanted was my parents.

"But..." I chewed my lip. "We don't want to go toward the exit, do we? I thought you wanted to go north?"

"We have to head toward the exit first. There was another tunnel branching off early on, we need to take that one."

"Well, I trust you. Lead the way!" Jenna said.

"Agreed." I scooped up the glow stick, then nearly jumped out of my skin when Blake tapped me on the shoulder.

"Can I have that?" he asked.

I looked at the glow stick in surprise and then handed it to him. "Sure."

"It's so pretty," he said under his breath. I think I'd scrambled his brain when I took him astral-walking, that was the only reason I could think of for his strange behavior. I'd have to talk to Gran about it when we got back, see what she thought.

"Let's go then." Remy turned right, and we followed. I dropped back, letting Blake move ahead of me, purely so I could keep an eye on him. I didn't trust that he wouldn't wander off or stop to look at something *pretty*.

Remy set a mean pace; I was actually sweating by the time we arrived at our destination.

"This is more like it," she said, hurrying across a wide cavern, her sharp eyes picking up something on the other side. I was standing, directing my torch at the roof of the cave, awed by its size, when lights flickered on.

"Lights?" My eyes snapped to Remy who was standing next to a spotlight on a metal frame, beneath it a large, square, battery. Next to it a folding chair and a box, a water bottle and a canvas tarp spread on the ground like a picnic rug. "Is this it?" I practically ran over, Jenna hot on my heels.

Remy was beaming. "This"—she indicated the surrounding items—"is your parents' setup. This is where they were working."

"Cool." Blake sprawled in the chair, a collection of glow sticks clasped in his fist. Remy raised a brow but said nothing.

"Your machine picking anything up?" I asked.

She held it out in front of her and walked the perimeter of the cave. The light was flashing, and she was reading the screen before returning to us with a puzzled look on her face. "It's going crazy. Like...they're here. They are standing here." She pointed the machine at the middle of the cave, and we all looked at the empty space.

"Mom? Dad?" I called, my voice echoing off the walls. Nothing. I walked toward the center of the cave, hands out, expecting to bump into some invisible barrier at any moment, but it didn't happen; I walked right through.

"This is weird," Remy said, frowning at her device before tapping the side. Hard. "Maybe it's on the fritz."

Seeing the disappointment on my face, Jenna wrapped an arm around my waist and squeezed. "Hey, the silver lining, we found where they were working."

"You're right." I nodded, swallowing my disappointment and squaring my shoulders. "So, what have we got?" I joined Remy who was rummaging in the box. She laid out a small pick, trowel, brush, the usual things I'd seen my parents use for excavating fossils and artifacts.

"How did they get all this in here?" Jenna asked. "It must've been heavy."

"They have a trolley," I said absently, pulling out a jacket my mother wore and hugging it to my face, breathing in her scent.

"It's not here now," Jenna pointed out, her torch seeking and finding the wheel marks the trolley had left.

I dropped the jacket back into the box when a notebook fell out of the pocket. Remy picked it up, slowly flicking through the pages. "Cool," she said, more to herself than to us.

"What is it?" I asked, and she glanced up at me.

"Your dad's notes. Your mom's were back in the trailer—this is the most recent one. But get this. They think this cave is an ante-chamber, and that"—she looked from the notebook to the cave, slowly turned, then pointed—"is the entry point to the next chamber."

"And is that where they think it is? The copper pyramid? Beyond that rock wall?" We both crossed to the wall in question and stood looking at it.

Remy ran her hands over it, frowning. "There's something I'm not seeing."

"Besides the fact that the trolley tracks go right up to that rock face and disappear?" Jenna commented, her torch shining on the marks in the dirt.

I gasped. "Do you think they could be on the other side? Trapped?" I raised my hands and pushed against the rock. It was cold, hard, and didn't budge.

"I guess it's possible." Remy studied the track marks. "Let's just say we can't rule anything out."

"I'm hungry," Blake complained from his spot sprawled in the chair. "Can we go now?"

"How about you come over here and help?" I snapped, and he looked at me with hurt eyes. Oh, good grief. It was like he was regressing, from a full-grown man to a child. Sullenly he got out of the chair and slinked his way over to us, clearly not happy.

"What?" he grumbled. Remy and I eyeballed each other. His weird behavior was escalating.

"Can you feel any magic?" I asked him, "Is there an energy field here?"

I hadn't been able to detect anything myself, but maybe Blake could pick it up. After all, his special gift as a fae was manipulating energy. He could use it as a weapon or a shield, so if anyone was using something similar, he should be able to identify it.

With an exaggerated sigh he popped a hip, rested one hand on it, and with a toss of his head placed his other hand against the rock face, rolled his eyes to the ceiling and appeared to concentrate. Dropping his hand, he said, "Got nothing. Can we go now?"

I looked to Remy. "Do you have everything you need?"

She nodded. "I'll take the notebook back with us. Just let me take some photos and then we can go." As she moved away, she whispered under her breath, "What is with him?"

I whispered back, "I think something happened when I used his magic to help me astral-walk. But I'd no idea that was possible, or what has happened. I will talk to Gran about it when we get back, see if we can't get him back to normal."

After finishing up at the caves we collected Gran and headed into town, surprised at the level of activity that greeted us when we pulled up outside the hotel.

"Finally!" Blake grumbled, glow sticks still clutched in his hand. "I'm starving." He headed into the hotel without waiting for us.

"I wonder what's going on?" Jenna asked, eyeballing the cars parked in the street. There had to be over fifty. On previous visits we'd be lucky if there were five. People gathered on the sidewalk, swatting flies and talking. I saw Petrina hurrying in our direction, her eyes red.

"Petrina? What's wrong?"

Wiping her fingers under her eyes, she drew in a shuddering breath. "Gosh, sorry." She sniffed. "You guys here for lunch? Manny is inside, he'll take care of you."

"Wait." I rested my hand on her arm. "What's happened?"

She hesitated for a second, then blurted, "Someone has murdered my friend Beth." Her voice wobbled and the tears she'd been trying to hold back overflowed.

"Oh, no!" I gasped, wrapping her in a hug, "I'm so sorry."

Remy and Jenna made comforting noises, rubbing their hands up and down Petrina's back in support and comfort. "What happened?" Jenna kept her voice low.

"I can't believe it." Petrina's whole body shook. "Why would someone do something so awful? That poor girl."

"What did they do?" Jenna pressed.

"Beth was getting married next month," Petrina told us, "She was so happy and so excited. And then this morning her fiancé found her. Stabbed."

"In the chest?" Jenna asked.

"Why yes? How did you know that?" Petrina sniffed, startled.

"Because one of the tourists at the caravan park was killed the same way," Jenna said.

Petrina slapped a hand over her mouth. "Oh, my goodness, that's right. That young fellow, one of the treasure hunters. He came into the hotel a lot. I think he was sweet on Kaylee."

"Oh?" Jenna prompted.

"Only his friend didn't like it. I'd seen them arguing a time or two. Well, I assume it was about Kaylee. I'd caught them out the back canoodling."

"Canoodling? As in kissing?"

Petrina nodded. "But this is awful. First him. Now Beth. Who could do this? And why?"

"That's what I'm trying to find out." The deep voice of Senior Sergeant Mick Gould startled us all. "Ladies," he greeted us, "can I remind you I need you to come to the station to go over your statements."

"We're just grabbing lunch and will be right over," Remy assured him. Petrina hurried away, wiping at her face as she did so.

"Two murders in two days," Mick said, studying us intently. "All around the time you lot arrive in town."

"What?" I gasped, hand to my chest. "You can't suspect us. We don't even know who this Beth woman is!"

"Just making an observation," he drawled, then touched a finger to the brim of his hat. "Make sure you swing by the station as soon as you're done. I wasn't kidding about those statements. And I have more questions."

Great. Now there had been another death—the

second stage of the ritual had been completed—and the local law enforcement thought we were suspects.

"I wonder if he's single?" Gran was watching Mick walk away, her eyes glued to his butt.

Shaking my head, I linked my arm with hers. "Come on, let's go eat. Blake isn't the only one who's starving."

TWELVE

Lunch was uneventful. The police station, not so much. Gran had set the tone by asking Mick if a) he was single, and b) would he be interested in a pole dancing demonstration. The look on his face had been priceless.

"You may need a chaperone when you interview her." I felt obliged to point out, "Gran has a thing for men in uniform. Who am I kidding? She has a thing for men in general."

"It's true." Gran winked, her thick lash extensions brushing her cheek. "You're the best thing about this whole trip."

Mick cleared his throat. "Maybe the two of you should come in together." He held the door open and Gran sauntered in ahead of me, making sure her shoulder brushed against his chest as she passed him.

"Sorry," I whispered, mortified.

By the time Mick sat opposite us he'd regained his composure. He opened a file, pulled out a sheet of paper and slid it across the table, then slid a different one toward Gran. "Read these. They are your statements from yesterday. Are they correct? Is there anything you want to add? Something you've remembered?"

I quickly scanned the typed-up page. "Remember how you asked me to check to see if anything else was missing from my parents' trailer?" I asked. He nodded. "Well....it may be nothing, but I found an empty ring box—and before you say anything, just know that my mom rarely wears jewelry. She will on special occasions, but day-to-day she doesn't."

"So, if she doesn't wear jewelry, why would her husband buy her any?" Mick asked.

"There was a note saying it was for their anniversary." I shrugged.

"So, you think someone has taken the ring? Diamonds, eh?"

But I was already shaking my head. "Not diamonds. An alexandrite gemstone."

Mick cocked his head. "But you don't know what this ring looks like? And you're certain she wasn't wearing it?"

"No. Sorry." He made a note on the bottom of my statement, then handed me a pen to sign it.

"So, I called Whitefall Cove Police last night," he said conversationally.

"You did?" I sat back, shocked. "Why?"

"Because I'm conducting a murder investigation," he said drolly.

Gran signed her statement and slid it back toward him. "And what did you discover?" she asked.

"It was quite enlightening." He sat back, crossing his arms over his chest. "You didn't mention you'd been arrested for murder." His eyes narrowed on Gran who merely shrugged as if it were a matter of no consequence.

"Those charges were dropped."

"Yet you were both involved in the investigation for the death of"—he paused, flicked the page in his notebook, briefly read whatever he'd scribbled there, and continued—"Whitney Sims and Bonnie Emerson. And here you are in Arrowstrand, with two murders since your arrival." He paused for dramatic effect. "Coincidence?"

"Absolutely coincidence!" I declared. "Who did you speak to at Whitefall Cove Police Station? Because if it was Officer Miles, well, she could be a tad biased."

Mick was shaking his head. "Nope. It was Detective Jackson Ward. Who, by the way, wants you to call him. Apparently, you've been ignoring his messages."

"Right," I muttered.

Gran was on it though. "Jackson has been calling?" A sly grin split her face, and I rolled my eyes. Here we go. Yes, Jackson had sent me some text messages I'd yet to read, let alone reply to.

"Harper had the misfortune to be engaged to an utter—" Gran began.

"Gran!" I cut her off before whatever vile word was about to spill from her lips would get us into trouble with law enforcement.

"Cad," she said, eyeballing me. "I'd been about to say cad. Geez, don't get your panties in a wad." She tossed her hair, well, tried to, but since Gran kept her hair short, there was nothing to toss so with a rather odd movement of her head, she continued, "Anyways, Harper moved back home to Whitefall Cove where she met the rather delicious detective. What is it with cops? You're all rather gorgeous looking. Is that a requirement?"

Mick blinked at her, but she continued on, not requiring a response. I could feel the heat rising in my face.

"Unfortunately for poor old Harps here, the detective is already taken, dating Officer Miles—is that even allowed? Fraternization among employees? Anyway, Harper has been pining after Jackson for months, biding her time I guess."

Oh, God! "Gran. Shut. Up." I growled, my face on fire. Why oh why did I bring her with me to Australia?

She ignored me, nothing new there. "But then Blake arrived. My lawyer." Gran fanned her face. "Phew-eeeee, that boy is hawt! And apparently single. And I felt for sure the two of them would—"

"Gran! Stop!" I shot out of my chair. Mick pointed at me and indicated I sit back down. I did. Slowly. He nodded once, then told Gran to continue.

"Harper seemed to like Blake, and Blake seemed to like Harper, but from the pent-up vibes I've been picking up from her I'd say things have stalled."

Mick's lips twitched, but he maintained a straight face. "And why do you think that is?" he asked, and I groaned. "Do you have to encourage her?" He shrugged. "I'm just curious."

"Here's what I think." Gran leaned forward, resting her elbows on the table. "I think Blake is a secretive chap. He's a mystery, an enigma. And that is freaking her out, you know 'cos her cheating ass fiancé was a liar and a cheat and she needs someone she can trust. Someone she can rely on. So, I think she put the brakes on because she's not sure she can trust Blake." She nodded. "He's very secretive."

Staring at her with wide eyes, I slowly blinked when it felt like my eyeballs were drying out.

"And also, she still has the hots for Jackson." Gran tacked on to the end and I buried my head in my hands, my humiliation complete. Silence ticked on for several moments before Mick cleared his throat and said, "Well, I suggest you give the detective a call, Harper. He seemed very keen to speak with you."

"Can we go now?" I asked without raising my head.

"Detective Ward also mentioned that you had some talent when it comes to investigations and that I shouldn't discount anything you discover."

This time I looked up. "What are you saying?"

"I'm saying that I doubt anything I say will convince you not to investigate these murders—especially because you think it relates to your parents' disappearance—so all I'm asking is that you be careful and keep me in the loop."

"You're okay with us helping?" I asked, shocked that I hadn't been told to butt out.

"This is a one-person police station," he pointed out. "With two murders in as many days, I'll take all the help I can get. But please, for the love of God, be discreet."

"Does that mean we're deputies now?" Gran asked hopefully.

"No, it does not." He handed me a business card. "Call me if you discover anything. Don't take any stupid risks. The station number will divert to my mobile if I'm not here."

"I will." I nodded, a little shell-shocked at this turn of events. "So... before we go, can I ask about the bodies?"

"Same MO. Hearts had been removed, a small rock with that circular pattern etched onto its surface in its place."

Mick didn't miss the look Gran and I exchanged. "What is it? You know something?"

I told him about our theory about the ritual, the sacrifices and the blood moon. I'd been expecting skepticism, but Mick just nodded, not surprised.

"You know about witchcraft?" I asked.

"I know someone has been up to something in this town lately. I guessed it was related to the occult."

"Why? What's been happening?"

"Dead animals, throats cut, remnants of black wax found at the scene. Bird feathers too. It all had a ritualistic feel to it. I've been searching online to see if I could find any information, a clue what this person was trying to achieve. And who it may be. Or even if it was more than one person." He lowered his voice. "Look, I wouldn't be telling you this if Ward hadn't vouched for you, so I'm counting on you to keep your heads down and not wind the locals up into a panicked frenzy. Think you can do that?"

I was affronted. Of course I wouldn't frighten the locals. As if. "Sure." I gave Gran the side eye. She'd better not let me down.

After everyone had given their statements and fingerprints, we'd returned to the trailer park. Blake, who'd been dozing in the car, stumbled out and staggered toward his cabin, mumbling something about taking a nap.

"Something is definitely up with him." Remy scratched her head.

"That reminds me." I grabbed Gran's arm. "Gran, could I have done this to Blake? I used his fae power to boost my magic to astral-walk. Ever since, Blake has been acting strange, definitely not himself."

Gran looked to Blake's retreating back, frowning in puzzlement. "I'm not entirely sure, love," she said. "Could be. We could ask the coven?"

"I may call Drixworths, see if Izzy knows."

"Good idea." Gran gave me a hug. "But Blake's got the right idea. A nap sounds wonderful. I'm beat."

"That just leaves the three of us," Jenna said, "What's the plan?"

I shrugged. "I've got some calls to make," I said. I'd been avoiding calling Jackson but now felt forced into it. Plus, I wanted to call Drixworths. Only it would be late in Whitefall Cove.

"I'm going to go through your dad's notebook," Remy said, pulling it from her backpack. "It may give us some clues."

"I'm going to update the murder board," Jenna said. "We know that Nigel led us astray in the caves.

And possibly moved the glow sticks, so we'd get lost down there. Although I don't think that was an attack on our lives, more a delaying technique. But to what end? He knows Remy is experienced, that she'd get us out."

"It may not have been Nigel who moved the glow sticks," Remy pointed out.

"You think Omar?" Jenna suggested and Remy shrugged, "Could be. I doubt either of them would actually tell us the truth though." Jenna and Remy continued their conversation as they headed into Remy's cabin.

"I'll join you in a few," I called after them. Jenna waved her hand in acknowledgement.

Blowing out a breath, I pulled out my phone and slid my thumb across the screen to unlock it. Another message from Jackson. He would not give up; he'd keep leaving me messages until I responded. Urgh, may as well rip the Band-Aid off. With any luck, he'd be asleep, and it would go straight to voice mail.

He picked up on the second ring.

"Hello?" His voice was groggy, heavy with sleep. "Harper?"

"Hi." Geez, titillating conversation there, Harper.

There was rustling, and I imagined him sitting up in bed. "Finally. I was getting worried."

"Pft, I'm sure Senior Sergeant Gould told you I was fine."

"Ahh, he told you we talked."

"Of course he did. Look, if you're calling to warn me to be careful, no need. I'm being careful." I didn't mean to snap, but my words definitely had a sting to them.

"Hey," he protested, voice gentle. "What's wrong, Harper? Why are you so defensive? I thought we were friends." There was a tinge of hurt to his words and now I felt like an utter bitch. I paced across the ground as I talked.

"Sorry." It wasn't much of an apology, but it was the best I could manage. It felt weird with him for some strange reason.

"What's wrong?" he pushed, his voice so deep and low in my ear, sending shivers down my spine. And in that moment, I realized I missed him. He was right. We'd become friends. Despite me having the hots for him, as Gran so eloquently put it, Jackson and I had formed a friendship and I'd been pushing him away ever since Blake arrived on the scene. And then I wondered if that had been Blake's intention, if he'd been manipulating me. My head was spinning.

I sighed, the sound whooshing down the phone to Jackson. I blurted out everything we knew, everything that had happened, the two deaths and the fear that tomorrow night, the night of the blood moon, my parents would be sacrificed. We were running out of time to find them.

"I wish I were there to help," Jackson said, and I smiled. I wished it too. With his necromancing powers he might be able to speak with Tamir and the murdered girl, Beth, find out who did this. But we didn't have the luxury of talking to ghosts at our disposal. "Look, when you get home, we need to talk. There's something I have to tell you."

"What is it? I figured it's important since you've been blowing up my phone with messages."

"It can wait."

A brief flare of irritation that he'd left a message at the police station for me to call him and now that I had he said it could wait? Men!

"Jackson, I have to go," I said instead. "Time is running out for my mom and dad."

"If there's anything I can do...."

"There isn't."

"Bye, Harper."

"Bye, Jackson."

I disconnected the call and stared at my phone. That was weird. But then everything was weird lately. You'd think I'd get used to it. Pulling up my contacts, I dialed Drixworths, intending to leave a message for Izzy.

"Oh!" I gasped in surprise. "I wasn't expecting you to be there. It's the middle of the night!"

"I've been expecting your call." I could hear the smile in her voice. Esmeralda Higginbottom—Izzy for short—was the headmistress of Drixworths Academy of Witchcraft and Wizardry and had taken me under her wing when I'd had my witch's license suspended. Now I had it back, she'd been working with me on controlling my magic. Apparently, I was a powerful witch and didn't even need a wand to use magic.

"Right. So, do you know why I'm calling?" I teased, testing her. I could picture her in my mind shaking her head and I chuckled.

"How can I help?" she asked instead.

I explained the situation with Blake. "I see," she said, her voice somber, and my heart stuttered a little. Had I damaged him? Injured his magic? "You would have been better placed boosting your magic with your Gran's and not that of a fae," Izzy told me. I bit my lip. It hadn't occurred to me at the time. He'd been there, he had magic, I hadn't stopped to think combining our power would hurt either of us.

"So why is it affecting him and not me?" I asked.

"Because you're stronger than he is." Well, that was a surprise—one I hadn't been expecting.

"But his symptoms? His behavior is almost childlike at times. Why? And how do I fix it?"

"You took a fae with you when you astral-walked, I assume to connect with your parents? Were you successful?"

"Yes. I connected with Mom."

"Right. I imagine then that somehow Blake has absorbed some of your mother's essence."

I remained silent for a second. "Say what?"

"He has...how do I put it?" Izzy paused while she searched for the right words. "He melded a little too closely with your mother. Now he has taken on some of her characteristics."

"But she doesn't act like a child," I protested.

"He may have inadvertently meshed with her inner child. Her memories of childhood, and now they are slowly taking root, growing stronger."

"How do I stop it? Is it reversible?"

"It took a great deal of magical power to make it happen in the first place," Izzy warned, "so it will take a great deal of magic to reverse it. You'll need your grandmother. And your familiar. And of course, Blake."

"I can do that. They're all here."

"This is what you need to do." Izzy rattled off a spell so fast I was lost after the first few words. "Don't worry. I'll text it to you. But please, once it's done, delete the text."

"I will, I promise." We said our goodbyes and hung up and, true to her word, Izzy sent through the incantation I'd need. Only problem was, we had to wait until midnight. Witching hour. And I feared midnight on the night of the blood moon would be curtains for Mom and Dad. I had a decision to make. Save them, or save Blake?

THIRTEEN

"We'll do both," Remy assured me when I told her of my dilemma. "Save your parents first, then help Blake."

"You make it sound easy." I sighed, sliding onto a chair at her kitchen table, suddenly exhausted.

"It is. Someone is holding your parents captive, right? We just have to figure out who."

"Okay." I nodded. "And how do we do that?"

Remy moved to the murder board. "We know Nigel deliberately led us astray in the caves, yes? So that makes him a suspect. And someone moved the glow sticks, possibly to delay us, throw us off our game."

"Right." I nodded.

"But something has been bugging me and I think I finally figured it out." She paced back and forth in front of the board. "When Tamir was killed, Kaylee found his body, right?"

"Right." Jenna nodded.

"And she said she'd gone into his cabin to clean it, that she'd used the master key after knocking and thinking he wasn't there, so it was safe for her to do her job."

"And?" I prompted.

"Where were the cleaning supplies?" Remy asked. I froze, my mind playing over the scene.

"There weren't any," I breathed.

"Right? She should have had a trolley or at least a basket or vacuum or something with her if she was there to clean his room."

"There weren't any of those things."

"So, you think Kaylee is the killer?" Jenna said dubiously.

Remy shrugged. "I'm saying she lied. I'm saying Nigel isn't the only suspect. Nor Omar. I think the two of them are in cahoots over the copper scroll and are trying to sabotage our attempts at finding your parents because they believe they know where the copper pyramid is and possibly the scroll too. They want to find it first. They just need time."

"We need to talk to Kaylee," Jenna declared.

Together the three of us headed up to the house. Andi heard the bell above the door jingle as we entered the reception area and came bustling through, an apron slung around her hips and her cheeks flushed.

"Oh, good morning." Her smile was genuine as she wiped her palms on the apron. "Sorry, I'm just doing some baking, I'm a bit hot and sweaty."

"Smells good." I sniffed the air appreciatively. Whatever she was baking smelled divine.

"Getting ready for Kaylee's birthday," Andi said. "Which reminds me, we're having a little get-together here, a casual barbie before Kaylee heads into town to celebrate with her friends. We'd love it if you'd join us. It'll just be us, Nigel and Omar. Oh, and Colin will be home."

"That sounds lovely, thank you." I smiled. "What time?"

"Six thirty?"

"Great. We'll be here." Remy turned side on to the counter and leaned her hip against it. "Is Kaylee about?"

"She's got a shift at the hotel today. Is there anything you need? Anything I can help you with?"

"Nah, that's okay, we were just going to wish her a happy birthday, but we'll see her tonight."

What better time to question everyone than when we had them all together in the one place? And we finally get to meet the elusive Colin. "Do you need us to bring anything?" I asked.

"Just your appetites."

Jenna snort laughed. "We can definitely do that." We bid farewell to Andi and made our way back outside.

"What should we do?" I asked the others. "Wait until this evening or...?"

"Time is not on our side," Jenna pointed out. "Let's head into town."

"What about Gran and Blake? Take them with us?"

Remy frowned. "They're both resting. Let's leave them to get their rest. Bandit and Archie will be here too. They should be fine."

I slipped a note under Gran's cabin door and the three of us piled into the Land Rover to head back into town.

"So..." Jenna waited until I was trapped in the car with no exit before she pounced. "Did you call Jackson?"

I nodded. "I did."

"And?" she prodded.

"And nothing. He said he had something to tell me when I get home."

She snorted. "So, he rings you to tell you he'll talk to you later. That makes no sense."

"I don't think he realized how crazy things were here." It only felt right that I defended him, a little.

"You know," Remy commented, "when a man acts that way, it's usually a matter of the heart."

Jenna gasped. "Do you think he's broken up with Liliana?"

"Why would he do that?" My words were automatic, no thought behind them.

"Duh, because he likes you. And you like him. Admit it, you always have." Jenna crowed with delight.

"It might not be anything like that at all," I felt compelled to point out. "Maybe he and Liliana are engaged, and he wants to tell me himself."

"Oh, shit," Jenna said. "That could work too."

"See? No point speculating," I told her.

"Remy, you seem to know Blake pretty well. What can you tell us about him?" Jenna switched gears so fast my head spun.

Remy raised one shoulder in half a shrug. "Not much. He's friends with my boss. Whenever he's in Australia he calls in to check up on the Bureau, other than that I don't see that much of him."

"What do you mean, check up on the Bureau?" Jenna frowned.

"His grandmother founded the Australian branch of the Bureau. Professor Elizabeth Tennant. She was pretty badass."

"Blake is a member of Bureau?" I hadn't known that—although it made sense that he was. It would explain a lot of things.

But Remy was shaking her head. "Nope. Not in the capacity you're thinking. The by-laws state a member of the Tennant family has to have a seat on the board and that's as far as Blake's involvement goes. Seb keeps him up-to-date with what's going on operationally, but Blake isn't an agent. He consults for us as a lawyer as and when we need it."

I remained silent pondering what Remy had just revealed. Blake's family were powerful. And obviously had connections around the world. It made it even more absurd that someone at his level would come to Whitefall Cove to represent Gran. And despite my best efforts I had unearthed no connection between Blake and my father, though Dad must know Blake to have called him when Gran was arrested.

Jenna sighed. "There's something attractive about a tall, dark, mysterious man."

Blake was all of those things, but I was starting to think Gran was right in her assessment. Blake was too secretive for me. Every question I asked was dodged, or half answered. I needed a man who would be truthful and honest. Although I liked to think Blake wasn't hiding the truth to be deliberately deceitful, maybe he thought he was protecting me, but still, after being lied to by Simon for over a year, I was leery of pursuing a relationship with a man who I knew was hiding something from me.

We arrived at the hotel, pulling me out of my musings.

"She's here." I followed the others to the bar.

Settling myself on a bar stool, I waited for Kaylee to finish serving a woman further down.

"Oh, hi, ladies." Recognizing us, she smiled. "What can I get you?"

"Beers?" Remy asked Jenna and me. We nodded. "Three beers."

"Will have to be stubbies." Kaylee nodded to the beer taps still covered by a tea towel. "Taps are out."

"That's fine. Tooheys if you have it."

"Coming right up." Kaylee expertly flicked the lids off of three bottles, then placed them in front of us along with three glasses.

Remy paid, then before Kaylee could move away, said, "Actually we'd like to talk to you if you have a minute?"

Kaylee looked surprised but nodded. "Oh. Sure. I guess."

"You discovered Tamir's body when you went to clean his cabin, right?"

"That's right." She nodded, her ponytail swinging.

"So where were the cleaning supplies?"

"What?" She frowned.

"There were no cleaning supplies in Tamir's room. Now I'd imagine if I discovered a dead body, I'd probably drop what I was holding. And from memory, you screamed. Loudly."

"I... err...." she stuttered, eyes darting away, "I don't know what you mean."

"It's only a matter of time before the police come to the same conclusion," Remy drawled. "Even faster if I go across the street and tell Mick myself." Remy moved as if to get up and do exactly that.

"No, wait!" Kaylee grabbed her wrist, preventing her from leaving. "Okay look." She dropped her voice, glanced around to make sure no one else could overhear. "The truth is, I wasn't there to clean. You're right."

"Why were you there?" Jenna asked.

Tears pooled in Kaylee's eyes. She sniffed. "Tamir and I were seeing each other. Only we were keeping it secret. My dad had already warned Tamir off. He'd seen him looking at me."

"Sooooo, you went to his cabin to hook up?" Jenna pressed.

Kaylee nodded. "Tamir said they were going to the caves first thing, and that I was to meet him in his cabin when he got back. He said he'd tell the others he was tired and needed a rest, that they'd buy it too because he looked tired, he had shadows beneath his eyes."

"And he was tired because the two of you...." Remy trailed off, eyebrows raised.

Kaylee nodded. "We spent the night together. Didn't get much sleep."

"So why meet up again so soon, if you'd already spent the night having all that sex?" I asked.

"Because Dad is due back today and it would be harder for us to meet up. Mom doesn't notice, but Dad? He'd know. Plus… it's my birthday. He said he had a present for me." She looked from me to Remy to Jenna, her eyes beseeching. "Please don't say anything."

"We're going to have to Kaylee," I replied, "It's a police investigation and if Mick is going to find Tamir's killer he needs to know the truth."

"Dad is going to kill me." She wailed, tears splashing down her cheeks.

I patted her hand. "I'm sure Mick will be discreet. You're an adult. You weren't doing anything illegal."

"I guess." She wiped her face and dragged in a shuddering breath. "So….you think I should tell Mick myself?"

"It would be better coming from you." Remy nodded.

Bowing her head in resignation, Kaylee blew out a breath. "Fine. I'll do it after my shift." Then she walked away.

I took a sip of beer. "Well, I didn't see that coming. Although now that I think about it, the night we arrived, Tamir was playing pool, and I saw Kaylee touch his leg. I didn't really think any more of it."

"I don't think any of us did." Jenna took a gulp of her drink, resting her elbows on the counter. "I wonder if Omar knew?"

"And Kaylee's dad," I said more to myself than the others. "He'd already warned Tamir away. Was it a father's intuition? Or did he know more?"

"But if he really was concerned that the two of them were sleeping together wouldn't he have told his wife? Warned Andi to keep an eye on them? And why was it such a big deal, anyway? Like you said, Kaylee's an adult and Tamir, okay, he was older but not by much, a few years."

"An overreaction on Dad's behalf, do you think?" Remy said.

I nodded. "Could be. I'm keen to talk to Colin— he's been absent in all of this, leaving Andi to handle everything, and considering these tours of his are only an hour away that's no excuse not to come home."

"Definitely weird," Jenna agreed. Then she gasped and turned to us, her eyes wide. "What if it's him? Colin. You said it Remy—he's been absent throughout all of this. What if he is holding Harper's parent's somewhere?"

I nodded in agreement. "It's definitely odd you don't come home despite one of your guests being murdered." A sense of foreboding danced up my spine. Tonight was the blood moon. If our suspicions were correct, whoever had my parents planned to sacrifice them tonight in the belief they'd become immortal, oh and let's not forget the part about great riches. Maybe they thought it'd show them where the copper pyramid was and the scroll. "Whoever doesn't turn up tonight," I said, talking to myself, "is the killer."

"What's that?" Jenna asked, and I jumped.

"Sorry, I was thinking out loud," I admitted.

"No, but you're right. You said whoever doesn't turn up tonight—I assume you mean to Kaylee's birthday barbeque—is the killer."

"They'd be getting ready for the ceremony. Their final sacrifice," I said.

"The most important one though, it has to be perfect," Remy cut in. "At the stroke of midnight. Under the rays of the blood moon. They'd have to control your parents and bring everything they needed, like a couple of hearts, candles, the glyphs."

"Wait! You said midnight? But... I need to cast Blake's spell at midnight. I can't be in two places at once." Panic was starting to rise.

Jenna clasped my hand. "Take a breath. Does Blake's need to happen tonight? Does it have to be a blood moon or just midnight?"

I sagged in relief. "He just needs it to be midnight," I said.

Jenna smiled. "There you go, he'll just have to wait until tomorrow night. It's all good." Then Jenna's smile slipped. "Now back to what Remy said. How would you subdue two adults? Drugs?" She swiveled to check out the patrons in the bar. "I wonder who you'd go to for drugs in this town?"

My beer hit the bar with a thunk. "You're right! They would have to be drugged. Mom and Dad are both very healthy, active, and strong people. They wouldn't go down without a fight. And they most certainly wouldn't cooperate in such a hair-brained situation."

"Right." I finished my beer in one long swallow. Wiping the back of my hand across my mouth, I told them, "Here's what we do. Jenna, I want you to ask around and see where you can score some drugs. As far as these people know you're just an American tourist. You could totally sell it that you're bored and looking for a buzz."

"And what will you be doing while I'm trying to score?" she asked.

"I'm going to talk to Mick, fill him in on what we've discovered so far. Remy, can you see what you can find out about Colin? Where his tours go, what he does when he's not conducting a tour, any gossip that we probably wouldn't otherwise hear out at the trailer park?"

"Let's do this!" Jenna grinned. We all fist bumped and then went our separate ways, agreeing to meet at the Land Rover in an hour.

CHAPTER

FOURTEEN

"I've got a lead." Remy was practically hopping from one foot to the other when we met at the Land Rover an hour later.

"Oh?" That was good news since my meeting with Mick had been a bust. He'd already figured out that Kaylee hadn't been at Tamir's cabin to clean it and he had her on his list of suspects to interview again.

"Apparently Nigel is in town, and he's really pissed off about something." She folded her arms and nodded her head in a *what do you think about that* gesture.

"I don't get it. How is that a lead?"

"Because Mrs. Butcher was filling up her car at the same time as Nigel was refueling his Ute—and let's not ignore the fact that we didn't know he had another vehicle! Where was he hiding that? I thought he only had the four-wheel drive he used to take us to the caves? Anyway, that's not the point. Mrs. Butcher said he was muttering and cursing under his breath. About Colin!"

That caught my interest. "What was he saying?"

"Something like 'That no good son of a bitch, I'm done saving his sorry ass.'"

"How long ago was this?" Pulling out my phone, I texted Jenna: *Get here NOW!*

"Not long. Ten minutes tops. Why?"

"We need to follow Nigel. I think he's going to Colin." It was a mad guess, but my gut told me I was right.

"But he'd have gone by now," Remy pointed out.

"Exactly. Which means we need to leave right now. Get in. This is a one road town. He either went east or west. We'll swing into the service station and ask."

"What about Jenna? We can't leave her behind."

"I'm here!" Jenna came rushing out of the hotel. "What's up?"

"Get in. I'll explain on the way."

Climbing into the Land Rover, I was still pulling on my seatbelt when Remy gunned the engine and pulled out with a spin of tires. I grinned. "I like your style."

"What's happening?" Jenna asked. I filled her in on what Remy had learned, and what had transpired at the police station. "How about you? Any word on where you can get drugs in this town?"

"Well, here's the interesting part." Jenna leaned

forward from where she sat in the rear seat and held onto the back of my seat. "There isn't a drug scene. The town is pretty clean. Word is if I want to score, I'd have more luck in Darana."

"Probably not enough business for someone to set up shop here," Remy agreed.

"But definitely easy enough to do," I said, "especially for someone who is on the road constantly."

"Geez, you don't think it's Colin, do you?" Remy snorted in disbelief. "Wouldn't that be funny! Not only is he smuggling drugs, but he's dealing in black magic too."

"You know that isn't such a stretch." I looked out the windscreen as Remy swung into the gas station. She jumped out, leaving the engine running.

"You've got a point," Jenna agreed. "If he's messing around with drugs it may have triggered a psychotic break. Some people are more susceptible than others, so maybe he takes a hit of cocaine and his mind creates this whole new world of immortal goddesses and vast treasures that are just his for the taking. All he has to do is kill a few people, and it's all his."

"And he's on the road a lot, he's his own boss, the tours could be the perfect cover."

"Do you think Nigel is involved in the drugs too?" Jenna wondered out loud. "He doesn't seem the type. But then they never do."

We both watched as Remy came hurrying back. I was shaking my head. "I agree, he doesn't seem the type, but then that's why he'd be perfect. Who would suspect him?"

"He headed west," Remy said, climbing in and slamming the door.

"Towards Darana." I nodded. The two towns were close enough you could do a roaring drug trade in both. But what if we were wrong? What if Colin had nothing to do with drugs and nothing to do with my parents' disappearance? Everything we'd discovered so far was circumstantial.

"Keep your eye out down the side roads," Remy instructed. "He may have turned off. Most of the roads are dirt, so you'll see the remnants of a dust cloud."

"Will do," I said. "I'll do this side, Jenna you do the right-hand side."

Jenna unclicked her belt and slid across the back seat until she was behind Remy, then re-did her seat belt, her gaze glued to the side window.

Nothing. We didn't see any sign of Nigel having turned off the main highway and here we were driving into Darana. It was bigger than Arrowstrand. The sign as we hit the city limits said Darana had a population of just over three thousand.

"Where could he be?" I chewed on the inside of my cheek as I tried to put myself in the shoes of a man I'd never met and didn't know that much about. It was an uncomfortable fit. "Nigel is looking for him... why? Why not phone him? Why drive all the way here?"

Jenna snapped her fingers. "Because his phone is off. Or the battery is dead. Or he's out of range."

I nodded. "So their communication is cut off. Which may explain why Colin didn't return home when Tamir was killed. Because he doesn't know. Although I'd imagine the local grapevine between Arrowstrand and Darana would work pretty well. Word should have reached him by now."

"Out of range then? He's not in town. He hasn't heard the gossip," Remy said.

"Did we miss it? Did Nigel turn off, and we missed the dust cloud because it had already subsided?" Jenna huffed, flopping back against her seat, disappointment clear on her face.

"Let's do a drive through, anyway," I suggested. "Keep your eyes peeled for Nigel's Ute."

We spent the next hour driving aimlessly around Darana, but there was no sign of Nigel or his Ute. Remy pulled up beneath a tree at a park on the outskirts of town. "It's a bust." Her frustration was equal to my own. Time was running out. I could practically hear a clock ticking in my head as the seconds counted down my parents' impending death. Needing to stretch my legs, I opened my door and was halfway out when Jenna squealed, "Oh my god! Is that him?"

"It is!" Remy yelled. "Hold tight!" The Land Rover was already moving as I swung my legs back in and I slammed the door.

Jenna was pointing, her finger jabbing the glass. "He came from down there!"

Nigel's Ute was at least two hundred meters away and he'd turned from a side street onto the main highway leading out of town. "He's heading back to Arrowstrand," Remy said.

"Which means he found Colin and delivered his message!" Jenna was bouncing up and down on the back seat and I couldn't hide the grin that tugged at my lips.

"Hang back Remy," I urged. "Don't let him see us." She eased her foot off the accelerator, and we watched as Nigel was soon a speck on the horizon.

Flicking on her indicator, she turned down the street he'd just come from. "This may be where the trail goes cold," she warned.

"Not necessarily. Remember that Colin takes tourists on four-wheel-drive tours. He's bound to have a logo or signage on his vehicle."

"You ever considered a career as an investigative reporter?" Jenna said. "Because you'd be darn good at it!"

"That's high praise coming from you." I chuckled. "But no, thank you, I'm happy with my bookstore. And as much as Australia is very interesting and beautiful, I'm looking forward to going home."

We drove slowly down the suburban street, past house after house until we were almost at the end and I'd been ready to admit defeat when I spotted it. A white four-wheel-drive with a sign on the door reading *Arrowstrand Scenic Tours*. Remy crept past while we all craned our necks and eyeballed the house where the vehicle was parked.

"Drive down further, then turn around," I said. "And stop. We'll watch from down the street."

"You think he'll leave?" Remy asked, doing as instructed.

"Yep. Nigel just delivered important news in person. We can only guess it was something along the lines of 'get your butt home.' And let's not forget it's his daughter's twenty-first birthday. But that means he would have been intending to return home today anyway, so why did Nigel hunt him down? Let's see whose house this is."

"Jenna's right. You are good at this." Remy turned off the ignition, pulled on the handbrake and we all watched out of the front windshield, waiting.

"I guess I've had a bit of practice." I shrugged. Two murders in Whitefall Cove since I'd returned home.

Officer Liliana Miles had said I attracted trouble, and I was starting to think she was right.

"Here we go," Remy murmured. We watched as a man in his late forties left the house. Colin Webb, I assumed. He was dressed in blue cargo shorts, boots, and a dark blue polo shirt stretched taught over a large belly. On his head a baseball cap. In his hand, an overnight bag. I cocked my head and watched as he opened the back door of his car and tossed the bag inside. So this was where he stayed when in Darana, supposedly for convenience's sake for his early and late tours. Then I saw the real reason. A young woman came out of the house, dressed in a flowing sundress, her long hair shining under the sun. She waited by the car and when Colin closed the door, he pulled her into his arms, planting a long, slow kiss.

"Oh god. I think I threw up in my mouth a little," Jenna choked. "He looks old enough to be her father. And look at her. She's gorgeous. What's she doing with an overweight middle-aged man? He's probably balding under that cap too."

"He does appear to be punching above his weight," Remy agreed.

I couldn't say a word. I was seething. *Dirty, rotten, cheating bastard.* Poor Andi. I knew what it felt like to be the one cheated on. I wondered if she suspected her husband was having an affair. It was easy from the outside looking in to assume there would be signs, but

I'd had no clue Simon had been maintaining an affair with one of his students right under my nose for a year. I'd had absolutely no clue. The remembered hurt and shame resurfaced, and I wanted to burst from the car and confront the pair.

"Easy, Harper." Jenna laid her hand on my shoulder when she saw me reach for the door handle. I let my hand drop. Colin ended the kiss and climbed into his four-wheel-drive, and waved an arm out the window as he reversed out the driveway and drove away. Back home to his wife. We continued to watch the woman who wound her hair on top of her head and secured it with a hair tie she had around her wrist.

"Christ, she doesn't look to be any older than Kaylee. I wonder if she knows he has a family in Arrowstrand?" Jenna said. I shrugged.

"Do we go talk to her?" Remy asked, fingers tapping on the steering wheel as she waited for instructions.

I looked from Remy to Jenna. "What do you think?"

"I think we should," Remy said. "We can't rule her out of this. She could be in it with Colin. What if your parents are here, in her house?" A very good, valid point.

"Okay. Let's do it." I opened my door and climbed out, Remy and Jenna following suit. We walked along the uneven footpath to the woman's house and knocked on the door.

"Hello?" We couldn't see through the mesh of the screen door.

"Hi." Remy reached into her back pocket and pulled out a badge, holding it up briefly. "My name's Remy Leigh, I'm an agent from Adelaide, and these are my associates. We're investigating the murders in Arrowstrand and were wondering if we could ask you some questions?" Oh, she was good. Enough detail to be convincing without actually lying.

"Oh yes, Nigel was just here telling us about what had happened." The screen door opened, and she ushered us inside. Her house was lovely with a quaint, hippy type vibe.

"What can I do to help?" Her worry and concern looked genuine, as did her youth. So damn young.

"Can we start with your name?" Jenna whipped out her phone and hit record.

"Of course. I'm Annabel Price."

"And the man who was just here, he's your boyfriend?" Remy asked.

Annabel nodded. "Yes. Colin Webb."

"What else can you tell us about him?"

She paled, her hand clutching at her throat. "You don't think he's involved, do you?"

"We're following up several lines of inquiry," Remy deadpanned. "So Colin lives here with you?"

"Yes. He stays overnight in Arrowstrand a few times a week because of his tours. Sunrise and sunset tours. It gets tiring traveling between the two towns so sometimes it's just easier if he stays over there, plus"—she blushed,—"he says I don't always let him get enough sleep when he's here."

I ground my teeth together but didn't say a word. He spun Annabel the same lie he told his wife, with neither being aware of the other.

"And who is Nigel?" Remy asked.

"He books the tours for Colin, like his tour manager, I guess. He dropped in today because he needed to talk to Colin about business and couldn't get him on the phone. That's when he told us about the deaths in Arrowstrand. It's truly awful." She wrung her hands together.

"Do you mind if I borrow your bathroom?" I asked.

"Oh, sure." We were standing in her living room and she pointed over her shoulder. "Off the kitchen is a hallway. It's the second door on your left."

"Thank you."

I left Jenna and Remy to continue the questioning of Annabel and headed down the hallway. Of course, I didn't have to use the bathroom—it was a ruse—but I opened the bathroom door, poked my head in, then silently closed it again. Tiptoeing down the hallway, I peeked into each room. No sign of my parents. No sign of witchcraft either, no altar or witch tools. If Colin had my parents, he wasn't holding them here. Creeping back to the bathroom, I flushed the toilet, ran the tap, then joined the others.

"Thanks for your cooperation, ma'am," Remy said. "We'll be in touch if we have any further questions." And with that we hustled out the front door and back to the Land Rover.

"Well?" Jenna hissed once we were inside the car.

"Nothing. They're not there. And the backyard is nothing but weeds. No garage or anything. What about you guys, she reveal anything else? Besides her so-called boyfriend is a cheating scumbag, that is."

"Nope. She said Nigel turned up, had a heated conversation with Colin out the front, then left. Colin told her he had to leave, told her about the murders and that he might be tied up in Arrowstrand for a while because, get this, the Arrowstrand Caravan Park was one of his biggest clients and they needed his support right now." Jenna sneered, her fingers mimicking air quotes.

"Let's head back. We know Colin's secret—not drugs, an affair. And Nigel knows his secret and is covering for him."

"Yeah, but he's not happy about it," Remy pointed out. "Mrs. Butcher said Nigel was furious when she saw him earlier."

"It will be interesting to see them together tonight

at the barbecue," Jenna said. "But also, we don't know who is peddling drugs in Arrowstrand."

"Maybe Kaylee would know?" I suggested. "She works behind the bar at the hotel. She's probably seen a few deals go down. See if you can bring it up in conversation with her tonight."

After freshening up, we headed to the house for the birthday celebrations. Andi was bustling between the kitchen and the rear deck where everyone was gathered. Colin was at the barbeque, tongs in hand. Nigel was at the far end of the deck, a cigarette clamped between his lips, Omar with him.

Kaylee arrived, looking frazzled. She paused by my side. "I spoke with Mick. He knows the full story. I'd appreciate it if you kept your mouth shut." She strutted off before I could answer. My eyes met Jenna's, and she quirked an eyebrow. I shrugged.

"I think we should split up," I said, keeping my voice low. "Gran, you go talk to Nigel. See what you can find out." We'd already filled Gran in with what had transpired today with Nigel's mad dash to Darana to warn Colin to come home. "Remy, you take Omar. He knows about the scroll; we can't discount he knows about summoning a goddess too."

"On it." Remy broke off, snatching up two beers from the cooler and approaching Omar with a smile, holding out a beer. His eyes registered his surprise, but he accepted the beer and clinked bottles with her before taking a swig.

"Jenna, try to get close to Kaylee," I said.

"Easy." Jenna nodded. "We struck up a bit of a friendship at the hotel today. Shouldn't be hard to pursue that further."

"Where's Blake?" I craned my head, finally spotting him ascending the staircase at the side of the house. I crossed to meet him. He would not be of much use investigative wise, but he was still an extra set of eyes. "There you are."

"Oh hey, Harper." His smile was wide and genuine.

"Hey, Blake, how are you feeling?"

"I'm good." He nodded, sliding his hands into the pockets of his jeans and rocking back and forth on his heels. "What's happening?"

I frowned. "We're celebrating Kaylee's birthday. Remember?"

"Oh yeah, I got that." He scoffed. "I meant, what's up? With you? You look sad."

I blinked. "I'm missing my mom and dad, that's all."

His jovial mood sobered. "Yeah. Your mom is great." I didn't know what to think. Did Blake actually know my mom, or was he reacting to the inadvertent mind meld he had with her?

"Will there be cake? I like cake." And he was off, following Andi inside

"And that leaves me with Colin," I said to myself, my eyes landing on the man turning sausages on the grill.

Dinner was a loud and raucous affair. The food was delicious and plentiful, and each of us was plying our respective charges with alcohol to loosen lips. So far it wasn't working. We had nothing and I could hear the tick tock of time running out.

Andi tapped the side of her glass with her fork to get our attention. She stood. "It's been lovely to have you all gathered here around our table." She smiled in genuine appreciation. "And I'm especially happy to have my husband home." She bestowed a loving hand on Colin's shoulder.

Sitting directly opposite, I met his eyes. He didn't blink, just stared blindly at me. *Yeah, you cheating bastard. I know what you did.*

Andi continued, "But most of all, we're here to wish our baby, our beautiful Kaylee, a happy birthday." She nudged Colin. "Sweetheart? Can you do a toast while I get the cake?"

"Oh. Sure." Colin snapped out of whatever daydream he'd been indulging in and stood, holding a beer in his hand.

Kaylee watched expectantly.

"Twenty-one years ago today, you came kicking and screaming into the world," he began, "and boy, did our lives change." He chuckled. "Let the sleep deprivation begin. Over the years we've watched you grow into the beautiful, wonderful young lady you are today, and your mother and I couldn't be prouder. I know you don't enjoy being the center of attention and I also know you're holding your breath and hoping I don't turn this speech into an embarrassing moment. Relax, baby girl, I've got you." He paused, checked over his shoulder to see Andi give the nod from the doorway. As she walked out with a birthday cake glowing with candles, Colin smiled and said, "Happy birthday, Kaylee."

We burst into song, all watching, enthralled as Andi set the cake in front of Kaylee. As the last "hip, hip hooray" faded, she blew out the candles. Andi dropped a kiss on her daughter's cheek and handed her the knife.

"Who wants a piece?" Kaylee asked, plunging the knife into the cake, expertly serving up slices of rich chocolate cake onto plates that Andi then passed around.

Colin continued to stare at me and I arched a brow at him. A dark flush of color ran up his collar and into his face. I had gotten little out of him in our conversation by the barbeque earlier. I'd pushed—hard—about his tours and my skepticism about needing to stay away from home because of them had crept in. I practically told him I knew he was having an affair, but it had been water off a duck's back. Until now. Now he seemed to be piecing it all together, the penny finally dropping. Which told me he wasn't the sharpest tool in the shed if it'd taken him this long.

After we ate the cake, the women helped gather the dishes and carry them to the kitchen. I caught sight of Colin grabbing Nigel's arm and dragging him down the stairs leading off the deck. Handing Jenna the stack of plates I was carrying, I hurried to follow, being as quiet as possible as I eased down the stairs. It was dark now; the sun had set with a magnificent display before dipping below the horizon and now the blood moon was dominant in the sky, casting more light than I'd like. Keeping my back pressed to the side of the house, I crept along until I spied the two men standing close together near the far corner of the house, voices low.

"How the hell would she know then?" Colin hissed, voice full of rage.

Nigel shrugged, putting another cigarette to his lips and cupping his hands around the end as he lit it. "How should I know? I told you, I haven't told anyone. How long do you think you can keep this up? I may have kept your secret, but it doesn't mean I approve. Andi is a good woman. She's stood by you throughout everything, yet you continue to lie to her."

"Shut up," Colin grumbled, grabbing Nigel's shirt in his fist. "You don't know anything."

"Oh, I know plenty," Nigel scoffed. "Not just about Annabel either."

"What do you mean?" Colin paused and Nigel pushed him away. There was a scuffle, Colin slammed Nigel up against the side of the house and I winced. "I said, what do you mean?" Colin's voice rose, carrying on the night air.

"I know about the fire," Nigel snarled. "And the missing drugs from the vet's bag."

Colin released his hold on Nigel and ran his hand around the back of his neck. "Well shit," he said.

"Exactly," Nigel spat. "So if you don't—" He was cut off by Andi calling Colin's name.

Shit. If she came down the stairs, she'd see me. I quickly swung beneath the staircase and crouched low to the ground, holding my breath and praying no one saw me.

The two men had frozen in place when they'd heard Andi call and now Colin spun on his heel, shouting, "Coming!" He climbed the stairs, his feet only inches from my head. Nigel watched, dragging on his cigarette before tossing it to the ground and grinding it out with his boot. He turned and headed toward the front of the house.

Darting out from behind the stairs, I followed.

CHAPTER
SIXTEEN

Keeping to the shadows as best I could, I followed as Nigel headed across the open expanse of the park towards his trailer. I mulled over what I'd overheard him say to Colin. He mentioned a fire. Was it the one that heralded the collapse of the sheep station? The one that destroyed the Webb family's homestead. I tried to remember if Andi had said anymore about the fire, what had caused it, because now I was thinking that maybe, just maybe, someone had lit it intentionally. And what was that about drugs being stolen from a vet's bag? I'd stumbled upon the idea that Mom and Dad had to have been drugged to make kidnapping them possible, but so far, we had found no one in Arrowstrand who had access to drugs—even the medical center where the visiting doctor ran his clinics was drug free. It seemed Nigel had the answers to all of my questions.

A sharp sting in the back of my thigh had me slapping at my leg. "Ow!" Damn mosquitoes. This wasn't the first time they had bitten me, but considering the little blood-sucking insect had managed to bite me through my jeans he must have been the size of a bush turkey. My fingers brushed against something, forcing the stinging pain to flare again. "What the hell?" Stopping, I twisted to try to see the back of my thigh, my fingers softly brushing over a foreign object sticking out. Was that... a dart? I plucked it from my leg, holding it up in front of my face, and peered at it in the dim light. It *was* a dart. A small one. I blinked, my vision turning hazy.

"Oh no. No, no, no." The realization that I'd been drugged hit me with the force of a sledgehammer. Of course it could have been whatever drug was in that dart, but nevertheless, my words were slurred, my vision blurred, and my limbs heavy. I was halfway between the main house and my trailer and I wasted precious seconds trying to decide which was my better option. Back to the house and the safety of others?

Or my trailer, where I could lock myself inside and hopefully sleep off whatever drug was rendering me incapacitated. I couldn't think, my brain was a fog, but my legs staggered onward with little control from me. When they gave out, I fell to my hands and knees and crawled. I had no idea my trailer was so far from the house, but when you're crawling over hard dirt everything seems a million miles away. My arms gave out, and I crashed to my chest, my chin hitting the ground with a thunk, my teeth rattling in my skull. Ouch.

I lay sprawled in the dirt, trying to think. I should call for help. Opening my mouth, I tried calling out, but nothing came out, just a feeble croak, my tongue swollen and thick. Then I heard it. Footsteps. Oh thank goodness, someone was coming, I was saved. I lay with my head resting on one arm and waited for my rescuer to reach me when a niggling thought popped into my ever so sluggish brain. *It's not your rescuer you idiot. It's the killer.*

Adrenaline spiked and with a burst of energy I began commando crawling, ignoring the bite of gravel tearing up my elbows. I was making great progress until a foot pressed down between my shoulder blades, pinning me to the ground.

"Not so fast."

I struggled to identify the voice. Was it Colin? I couldn't be sure. My eyelids were so heavy I couldn't open them, and I was sliding deeper under the effects of the drug. The pressure on my back eased, but I couldn't take advantage, I couldn't move. With a sigh, I gave in and darkness claimed me.

Urgh. Mother of God, my head hurt. I stirred, the drumming inside my skull relentless. And my mouth was dry, drier than a dessert. Must have been one hell of a bender. I went to roll out of bed and that's when I discovered I couldn't move. A brief flash of panic shot through me. Was I paralyzed? Cracking open an eye I frowned at the corrugated iron filling my vision. I wasn't in my trailer. Where the hell was I? As I blinked my eyes and my vision sharpened, I moved my head to take in more of the room where I was being held. It was slowly coming back. Someone had drugged me.

"She's waking up."

"Mom?" I swung my head too fast and the whole room spun, making me want to hurl. Quickly squeezing my eyes shut, I sucked in a deep breath through my nose and held it, feeling my lungs expand, before slowly releasing it, feeling the nausea abate.

"It's okay, honey." Dad's voice. Slowly I opened my eyes again. Sitting next to me, tied to their chairs, were Mom and Dad. I sagged in relief. They were alive.

"Harper?" My attention zeroed in on my mother and I gave her a weak smile. My happiness at seeing them was tempered with feeling like death thanks to the drugs in my system. "Mom? Dad?" I croaked.

"Don't talk," Mom said. "They drugged you. It'll take a while to fully leave your system."

I nodded and then wished I hadn't, as another wave of nausea descended. This time I couldn't stem the tide and I hurled all over the floor in front of me. I tried to free my arms, but they were zip tied to the arms of the chair, as were my ankles. I coughed and then spat, hating the taste of vomit in my mouth. "Sorry," I croaked.

"Don't be," Mom soothed. I could hear Mom and Dad softly talking to each other, couldn't make out the words, and I must have dozed off because the next thing I knew water was being poured over my head. I woke with a gasp, coughing and spluttering. Through my dripping hair I saw Kaylee holding a bottle of water over me, a sneer on her face.

"Awake yet?"

"Kaylee?" I hated to state the obvious, but in my defense I'd just been drugged and wasn't exactly thinking straight.

Satisfied I was awake, Kaylee tossed the now empty water bottle and grabbed another one from a table shoved up against the wall. She poured it over the puddle of vomit, and I watched as it washed away between the gaps in the floorboards. My eyes traveled along the floor. How odd. There was a sizeable gap between each board and beneath us, through the gaps, a long way down, was dirt. Looking up, I finally took stock of my surroundings. A shed. A big, shed. It smelled funny. There were pens and a large round table.

"Where are we?" I asked.

"The old Arrowstrand Station shearing shed," Kaylee replied, rummaging inside the backpack she'd tossed onto the bench next to the lined up water bottles.

"Is that what I can smell? Sheep?"

"Probably. Now shut up. No talking."

I glanced to Mom and Dad who were frowning at me and jerking their heads toward Kaylee. I raised my brows. *What? You want me to shut up or you want me to stop her?* Since I wasn't in a position to stop her, I elected to shut up. Keeping one eye on Kaylee, I wriggled my wrists, trying to slide them free from the cable ties, but it was no use, they were on good and tight.

"Sorry," I said, not being able to sit in silence, "but I've just got to ask, how did you get my parents here with no one noticing?"

Kaylee shot me a look over her shoulder. "Same way I got you."

"But where did you get the drugs? And what were they, because I feel like shit?"

She shrugged, placing a black candle on the bench, followed by a silver dagger. "Horse tranquillizers. Don't worry, I didn't give you a full dose. That would've killed you and I need you alive. For now."

"So it was you..." Nigel had been talking about Kaylee. Kaylee had stolen the tranquillizers from the vet's bag. He must have been visiting the sheep station when it was still operating, administering to a sick animal, and Kaylee... what? Had the foresight that one day she'd need a powerful tranquilizer?

Kaylee shrugged, not caring about what I had to say.

"Did you set fire to the homestead?" I asked.

That caught her attention. She turned, leaned back against the bench and crossed her arms over her chest. "Aren't you the clever one?" There was such a lack of emotion on her face, it was creepy. Her eyes, that had always seemed so blue, were uncannily dark, although it could have been the light in the shearing shed. A single lantern was dangling overhead. "We wanted out. It was the best way." She shrugged again and then turned her attention back to her bag of tricks.

"We?" Was the whole family in on it? Burn down the homestead for the insurance money?

"Enough talking!" She spun and threw something at me and for a split second I thought it was the dagger, thought I was about to die. It was almost a relief when an apple bounced off my chest and rolled to the floor.

"Harper," Mom warned. "Shush."

"You'd better listen to mommy dearest." This time Kaylee picked up the dagger, and I froze, not daring to breathe. She pointed the dagger at me, and I sat there, silent, unable to breathe until she nodded in satisfaction and put the dagger back on the bench. "That's better."

"We're almost ready folks!" Suddenly she was animated. The dull, lifeless face was replaced with sparkling eyes and curled lips. "I'll be right back." I listened as her footfalls faded into the distance, the sound of a metal door sliding open.

"What's going on?" Mom asked. "What does she have planned?"

"She didn't tell you?" It surprised me. I was sure Kaylee was sadistic enough to have rubbed it in their faces but seeing their confusion she obviously hadn't. "She intends to summon the Goddess of Immortality." I explained. "She's doing a blood ritual, and tonight is her grand finale."

"Dark magic," Mom hissed.

"Sounds bad," Dad added.

"It's very bad. She's already killed?" Mom questioned me, her eyes, so much like mine, were sharp and alert.

I nodded. "Twice. One male, one female."

Mom thought for a second. "I'm guessing she found my ring?"

"The alexandrite one? Yes. How did she even know about it?"

"We were talking about marriage and

anniversaries in the hotel at dinner one night, Andi and Colin were there too, and your dad was teasing me that he'd bought me this ring for our anniversary, but it never saw the light of day."

"And Kaylee overheard."

Mom nodded. "She must have. She was working."

"How do we stop her? Can you use your magic?"

Mom was shaking her head. "I don't have my wand, and you know I rarely practice. But Gran tells me you're doing really well with your magic, Harper." Mom smiled softly at me. "That you don't even need a wand."

"Wait," Dad interrupted, "does Kaylee know you two are witches?"

"I don't think so," I said. "It's not something we talk openly about, not amongst strangers. And Remy said that whoever it was that was practicing dark magic was not a witch, but human. Remy has some sort of gadget that reads energy signatures or something." I couldn't recall all of the details as most of the explanation that Remy had given me had gone straight over my head.

"Remy's here?"

"Yes. And Dad, Blake Tennant is here too. He got Gran cleared of all charges—well actually, we found the real killer which meant they dropped the charges."

"I knew he would." There was a level of pride in Dad's voice, which prompted me to ask, "How do you know him? He works for Richards, Jones & Tennant and apparently the Jones is a silent partner. Is that you?"

Dad was silent for a moment and suddenly the ridiculousness of my question wasn't so ridiculous anymore. "Dad?"

"Keith, tell her. She deserves to know," Mom urged him.

"You're right, of course you're right." He blew out a breath, cleared his throat then said, "Yes, I'm the silent partner in Richards, Jones & Tennant. I have a law degree but never practiced."

"But... why? Why even be a partner if you don't practice? I don't understand."

"You mentioned the Bureau," Dad replied, then paused. "The Tennant family formed the Bureau in Australia after the SIA was formed in America."

I nodded. "Blake mentioned something about his sister working for the SIA."

"Right. So both organizations work hand in hand in keeping supernaturals legal."

"But what does that have to do with you? You're human."

"Well, you know Grandpa was a lawyer. And his dad before him. So of course, it was expected that I'd follow in their footsteps and I did, went to law school, graduated. Then I met your mom and for the first time I was exposed to the world of the paranormal."

"Riiiiggghhhhtttt." I had no clue where this was going.

"And it was then I discovered that my dad had worked with the SIA when they were first founded, helped them establish their infrastructure, their laws and punishments, etc."

I sat in silence, my mind slowly turning over what he'd said. I wished like hell I wasn't still feeling the effects of the drug Kaylee had shot into me.

"What he's saying," Mom cut in, "is that your dad's family has been involved in the supernatural world for a long time, and that when Dad got out of law, he still kept a foot in that camp by becoming a silent partner in the law firm."

"So why the secrecy? Why couldn't Blake have just told me this? He said you were friends, that you went way back, but he refused to tell me anything else."

"Because we have a code of conduct just like everyone else and he couldn't tell you what you wanted to know. It wasn't his secret to tell."

We heard movement outside and Mom said in a rush, "Harper, I want you to try to use your power to push the toxins out of your body. I know you feel like crap right now and it's impeding your magic, but you are our only shot to get out of this alive."

"Why?" Dad asked. "What's Kaylee going to do?"

"She's going to sacrifice us," Mom told him. "She's already killed two people to reach this goal and now that I know what she wants, it makes perfect sense. She'd already targeted us as her final sacrifice—two hearts in love. But she needed to wait until the night of the blood moon to kill us."

"Only we would not be around." Dad nodded, the penny dropping. "We were going home."

"Exactly. She couldn't afford to let us go. I don't think there are many residents in Arrowstrand who would qualify as truly being in love."

I snorted. "Got that right. Did you know Colin has a second home complete with a younger woman in Darana?"

"Doesn't surprise me," Mom said. "I got a vibe from him from day one."

A car door slammed outside. "Enough chitchat," Mom whispered. "Harper, draw on your magic. Close your eyes and focus. She'll think you're sleeping and won't suspect."

My mind was a blank. "Then what?" I whispered back. "How do I free us? How do I stop her?"

"A protection spell first. Then break these cable ties. Your dad and I will take care of her if you can get us that far. Do you think you can do that?"

"I'll try." Closing my eyes, I concentrated on my magic, but it was sluggish to respond, slow and disobedient. It felt as crappy as I did.

"Look what I found skulking around outside," Kaylee crowed.

My eyes popped open when I recognized the outraged yowl of Archie. No! She couldn't have my cat, could she? I turned my head to see her holding Archie by the scruff of his neck, avoiding the claws he swiped at her. Oh my God, she was going to kill my cat, and I was powerless to stop her.

SEVENTEEN

"Archie!" I cried, tears welling in my eyes. He howled, long and loud. Kaylee jerked her arm, and he dangled there in the air, his legs kicking but not connecting. His golden eyes were black, his ears flat against his head. She crossed to the bench and picked up the dagger and I couldn't have it.

I couldn't let her gut my cat. My sluggish magic awoke, sensing the danger of my familiar. It rose within me, ricocheting through my body, burning through my veins. Narrowing my eyes, I focused on Kaylee, on the dagger in her hand. I made the dagger burn hot. It startled Kaylee, and she dropped it, crying out when it slipped through the gaps in the floorboards to fall to the earth below.

"Damn it!" she yelled, tossing Archie aside. He flew through the air, twisting as he did, to land on his feet, hackles raised. "I'll deal with you later," she spat at him, rushing back out the door, appearing beneath us minutes later.

"Archie," I whispered. "Come here. I need us all to be close if I'm to protect us all."

He blinked, then slowly slinked over to sit under my chair, bumping the back of my calf with his head. Having him near helped flush the toxins of the drug from my system even faster. I could only assume my cat had hitched a ride in the car Kaylee had used to bring me out here. Smart cat. I hoped that Bandit noticed Archie was gone and raised the alarm.

Closing my eyes once more, I concentrated on allowing my magic to increase, for my power to build on itself until I felt I would burst at the seams. I held it for as long as I could, then cast it, like a giant bubble, out and over Mom, Dad, me and Archie. Now I just needed it to hold while I worked on getting our bindings loose. It would be tricky to hold the protection spell while simultaneously working on another. From my peripheral vision I saw Kaylee under the shearing shed swipe up the dagger and then move out of sight. On her way back.

"Come on, hurry up." I heard her voice from behind, heard the door sliding open and then closed again. Who was she talking to? Did she have an accomplice?

"Well, if you didn't waste time messing about with

that damn cat we could be done already," Colin grumbled, coming into my line of sight. He was carrying a red cooler with chains stacked on the lid. My eyes widened at the realization they were working together, but I couldn't let myself get distracted. The protection spell was holding steady—I just needed to get our hands free. I focused on Dad first; he was physically the strongest.

"Put the Esky there. It'll make a good altar." She pointed and Colin set the cooler down directly in front of us. Picking up the chains, he eyed the beams above our heads, then with a grunt, tossed one end of the chain up toward the ceiling. It flew over the beam and he caught the other side as it swung by. "Still got it." He smiled to himself. Kaylee lifted two plastic containers from the cooler and placed them on the bench, then she covered the cooler with a black cloth, placed the dagger, the containers and a small drawstring pouch on top.

"Which one first?" Colin asked, his face gleeful.

"The mom." Kaylee pointed. "The men mourn the women harder. His heart will be full of love when he dies."

"His heart will be full of rage," Mom snapped, "and that'll ruin your spell, stupid girl."

"Hey!" Colin straightened and took a threatening step forward. "Don't you be calling my girl stupid! She's brilliant."

"Hardly," Mom scoffed. Good. She was keeping the attention on her, away from Dad, where I was valiantly trying to loosen the zip ties around his wrists. From the corner of my eye, I saw him flex his fingers into a fist and then relax. Was it working? Were they loosening? I didn't have much time. Once they realized they couldn't touch us through the protection spell I'd have to redirect my power back to reinforcing the spell and we'd be at a catch twenty-two. I couldn't divert my magic to loosen our bonds, and with our hands tied we couldn't defeat them.

"We'll chain them both up at the same time," Kaylee told her dad. "I'll get the mom, you get the dad." I noticed how Kaylee didn't refer to mom and dad by their names, as if she were distancing herself from the fact they were people and she was about to murder them. I wondered if growing up on a sheep station where animals were routinely slaughtered had damaged Kaylee's psyche, for I couldn't help but notice the dark-stained wood over a particular spot in the shearing shed. Sheep had died here. She fully intended for us to die here too.

Well, not today, not if I had anything to do with it.

Both Kaylee and her dad stepped forward, ran into the power of my protection spell and staggered back, confused.

"Hey!" Colin protested, stepping forward again only to be forced back. As predicted, I felt the dip in my magic at his attack on the perimeter and I closed my eyes, channeling more energy into the shield, while all the while trying desperately to loosen the zip ties.

Then it happened. Dad was free, the ties from his hands and ankles fell to the floor and he lunged at Colin with a roar, the two of them toppling to the ground. Taking advantage of the chaos and confusion I let the protection spell drop, just long enough to get Mom and me free, then flinging my arm toward Kaylee, I hit her with a bolt of magic, sending her scooting backwards and pinned to the wall.

"You all right, Dad?" I asked, feet braced as I kept one arm raised toward Kaylee and the other, pointed toward Dad and Colin where they wrestled on the floor.

"Do it," Dad grunted, rolling out of the way. I hit Colin with a bolt and seconds later he was pinned to the wall beside his daughter.

"Oh my God!" Kaylee cried in delight. "She's got magic! We should have killed her first and drained it. The Goddess would surely love such a sacrifice."

"Doesn't work like that, dipshit," Remy said from the doorway. I almost released my hold on the two of them as I sagged in relief. The cavalry had arrived. Remy hurried across the floor to my side. "Mick is seconds behind me. Lower them to the floor," she whispered in my ear. Right. Don't reveal my magic to the human. I did as instructed, lowering Colin and Kaylee to the floor.

"Professor Jones." Remy held out a hand to my father and helped him to his feet. "Help me restrain them."

"On it."

Remy positioned herself behind Kaylee and seized her arms, pulling them tight behind her back. My dad repeated the movement with Colin, but I kept my magic in place, just in case, only to any human onlookers, they wouldn't know it involved magic.

The next thing I knew, the shearing shed was full of people. My God, had the whole town turned up? Gran, Jenna and Blake, plus Andi, Nigel and even Omar. Mick cuffed Colin and made good use of our discarded cable ties on Kaylee.

"How did you find us?" I asked Remy, my legs wobbly now I'd let go of my hold on my magic.

"Bandit and Archie." She grinned. "I'm guessing Archie jumped in the back of the Ute when he saw you being taken, and Bandit saw the Ute leave with Archie in the back. He kicked up a ruckus, barking and howling and running down the road, so we followed. When I realized he was leading us down the road that led to the old homestead, I phoned Mick."

"The Ute? Nigel's Ute?" I frowned.

Nigel shuffled forward. "It's the old communal Ute from when the sheep station was in business."

"Did you know about this?" I demanded.

Nigel held his hands up. "I didn't, I swear. I mean, I knew Kaylee was fooling around with Tamir."

"What?" Colin spluttered. "I told you to stay away from him," he ground out, eyes latched on Kaylee, who shrugged, "Like you stayed away from sweet, sweet Annabel?"

"What's going on?" Andi cried, her face wet with tears. "I don't understand. Colin? Kaylee? What's happening?"

Remy put an arm around Andi's shoulders in comfort. "It's really a bit out there and hard to believe, but Kaylee has been practicing black magic," she told her.

"What? Black magic? But why? I didn't even know that was a thing... beyond TV shows and movies, that is." Andi wiped her nose on the hem of her T-shirt.

"She believes that she can summon a goddess who will make her immortal. Only black magic requires blood sacrifices."

"Are you telling me..." Andi swallowed and looked at Remy, her face fearful. "Are you telling me Kaylee killed that lovely young man, Tamir?"

Mick nodded. "She did. And Beth. And she was about to kill Mr. and Mrs. Jones. And probably Harper too just to keep her quiet."

Andi sniffed, then looked to Colin. "And you knew?

You helped her? And who is Annabel? Another girl you killed?"

Kaylee laughed, a note of hysteria tinging her voice. "Whose idea do you think this all was?" She jerked her head. "The old homestead? That was his idea. Burn it down, be done with it. Start afresh. Only you wouldn't leave Arrowstrand." Kaylee turned her nose up in the air. "So he was stuck here. With you. Until he met her. Annabel. Young. Pretty."

"What is she saying?" Andi whispered, her eyes beseeching her husband to deny what his daughter was telling her.

Colin ducked his head, mute and Kaylee scoffed, "See, Mom. He's weak. Just like you are. I mean, my god, how clueless can you be that he's been having an affair practically under your nose and you just merrily go about living your life, raising baby joeys, oblivious to what is going on around you. Dad hates it here. Always has. When Pop finally kicked the bucket, Dad saw it as his opportunity to sell up and move, but you loved it here and wouldn't let him."

"To be truthful"—Colin raised his head and pinned his daughter with a hard stare—"the fire was an accident. A happy one. *She* was practicing magic and accidentally set the kitchen on fire."

Andi looked from one to the other with wide, dazed eyes. "I don't even know you," she whispered. "My own husband and daughter are strangers to me.

What is *wrong* with you people?" Her voice rose in anguish and Mick jerked on Colin's handcuffs.

"Okay. That's enough. Let's go." He pushed Colin and Kaylee ahead of him and out the door.

Mom and Dad both wrapped me in a bear hug, and I hugged them back. "I'm so glad you're okay." I sniffed, my relief overwhelming.

"Come here, family." Gran sniffed, joining in our group hug and before I knew it Jenna and Remy were in on it too.

"Now what?" Jenna asked.

"Well," Gran drawled, "I do think it's time we got Blake sorted out, don't you? It's not midnight yet, we've got time."

"Let's do it." I nodded, but Gran was shaking her head at me.

"You didn't read the spell properly," she chided. "Besides saying the incantation at midnight, Blake also needs to be submerged in water."

I rolled my eyes in disbelief. So close, yet so far.

"To the swimming hole!" Remy declared.

EIGHTEEN

I basked in the company of my parents on the drive back to the caravan park. Sandwiched between them on the back seat, I held each of their hands, beyond grateful I had them back, whole and unharmed.

Mom yawned. "I'm really looking forward to a shower."

"Me too. And a decent night's sleep," Dad added.

"Did she keep you tied to those chairs the entire time?" I asked, my anger bubbling to the surface, only to subside when dad shook his head, "No, we were chained in one of the sheep pens most of the time."

"We're here." Remy pulled up right outside the trailer and we climbed out. "I'll meet y'all at the swimming hole," she said before driving off.

"I'll just grab my gear and get changed in Jenna's

cabin," I said to Mom and Dad, knowing they were looking forward to getting cleaned up and some much-needed rest.

"You can stay with us if you like, darling," Mom offered. "The kitchen table folds down and converts into another bed."

"That's okay, Mom," I said. "You deserve privacy after everything you've been through. I'll see you in the morning."

I gathered my bags, hugged them goodbye, then hurried to Jenna's cabin, catching her as she was leaving.

"Can I stay with you?" I asked. She'd just closed the door but promptly opened it again, holding it wide.

"Of course you can. As long as you don't mind a bunk bed."

"I don't mind at all."

After changing into my swimsuit, I grabbed a towel and slid my feet into flip-flops I headed toward the swimming hole with Jenna, lips curling in anticipation. I was fully recovered from the drugs and since I hadn't had the chance to experience the swimming hole yet I was looking forward to it. Not to mention my conscience would feel clear once we got Blake back to his usual self. I felt awful my magic had harmed him, as unintentional as it was.

The blood moon hung big and bright in the sky,

illuminating the way. We'd missed the actual eclipse, and all was back to normal. Well, relatively normal. I shivered a little in the night air and wrapped my towel around my shoulders for warmth. Rounding the corner of the house, I paused for a moment, watching in awe as water thundered down the rock face, the waterfall splashing into the pool below where Blake frolicked as if he didn't have a care in the world.

My eyes narrowed when I noticed Archie. He was actually in the swimming hole, swimming. I hurried forward, thinking he was in trouble, that he'd fallen in accidentally, only to skid to a halt when he climbed out, shook himself off, then promptly turned around and launched himself back into the water, executing a perfect feline belly flop. Bandit barked, then followed him in.

"Well, now I've seen it all," Remy drawled, coming up behind me. "A swimming cat."

I was shaking my head in surprise. "I had no idea."

A few feet from the swimming hole was a picnic table, and I tossed my towel on it before heading to where Gran was sitting on a ledge submerged in the water. Leaving my flip-flops at the water's edge, I eased myself in, gasping at the coldness.

"You get used to it," Gran told me, scooting over so I could sit next to her.

"Pft, you're doing it wrong," Remy scoffed, then launched herself into the air, clutched her knees to her chest, wrapped both arms around them, then crashed into the water, sending a giant wave all over us.

"Cannonball!" Blake shouted, swimming across the water hole to climb out and mimic Remy's efforts. Within seconds I was absolutely soaked. I may as well have dived in from the get-go.

Wiping the water from my face, I turned to Gran. "What's the plan for Blake?"

"It's a cleansing spell, and since we need to submerge him in water, I figured this is the perfect place."

Jenna joined us, sucking in a startled breath when she eased herself into the water. "Hooley dooley," she squeaked, "I wasn't expecting it to be quite so..."

"Refreshing?" I laughed. "It's okay. You get used to it."

"We should do this," Gran said, watching Blake as he dove to the bottom of the pool and then torpedoed himself up and out of the water.

"Can we help?" Remy had overheard and was already making her way to where we were sitting, half submerged.

Gran nodded. "Yes. It's a simple enough spell. I won't need you for the spell itself though. Since it was Harper's magic that messed him up, I need her to call her magic back."

"Tell me what I need to do," I said. Despite having

briefly read the spell Izzy had sent, I couldn't recall the details.

"We're going to enclose Blake in a circle," Gran explained. "And I'll cast the spell. I want you to focus on drawing your magic back to you."

I nodded. "I can do that."

"I'll do the incantation," Gran said, then nodded at Remy. "When I let go of Harper's hands, Jenna and Remy, I need you to push Blake under the water."

Archie shook himself, water flying from his fur, before coming to sit on the rock ledge behind us, lending his support to my magic.

Gran slid off the rock she'd been sitting on and swam to the middle. I followed. Holding hands and treading water would not be as easy as I thought, and I looked at Gran with concern. She was an old woman; did she have the strength for this? Seemed Jenna had the same thought for she followed and took up a position behind Gran, giving me a slight nod. I relaxed a little knowing Jenna was there to lend support should Gran need it. Remy took up a position just to my left.

"Ready?" Gran asked.

I nodded. "Hey, Blake, come on over here for a sec," I called.

He ducked under and swam toward me, popping up just in front of my face with a grin.

"We're going to play a game," I told him. "Kinda like ring around the rosy. Did you ever play that when you were a kid?"

"The one where you held hands and went around in a circle?" He cocked his head quizzically.

"Yeah, that one. Gran and I are going to make a circle, with you in the middle. But you have to stay there, okay?"

His face split into a big smile. "Sure! This sounds like fun." He obediently stayed put while Gran and I reached an arm either side of him, clasping our hands together and kicking our legs to stay above water.

Gran started the incantation and Blake snapped his head around to look at her, concern pulling his brows together. "What's happening?" he asked.

I shook my head at him, focusing on pulling any of my residual magic from him. I couldn't feel it, so I wasn't sure if I was doing it right or not, but Gran released my hands and said, "Now!"

Remy and Jenna placed their hands on Blake's shoulders and shoved him underwater, his protesting gasp cut off.

"Let him go." Gran was already swimming back to the ledge, and I followed to make sure she was okay. I heard Blake surface behind me.

"What the hell?" he demanded. "What did you do that for?"

The four of us looked at each other. Had it worked?

His voice had lost the childish lilt but that could be because he was angry we'd dunked him.

"What happened?" He swam to the edge of the swimming hole and hauled himself out, stood dripping in the moonlight, face shadowed so I couldn't tell what he was thinking. Or feeling.

"Do you remember helping me to astral-walk?" I asked, climbing out of the water. Goosebumps popped up on my skin and I shivered. I hurried to the picnic table and snatched up my towel.

"I do." He gave one nod, but other than that, hadn't moved. He must be freezing but didn't give any indication he felt the cold.

"Well, something that neither of us considered a possibility... happened," I admitted. "You sort of got pulled into my mom's psyche, developed some of her... traits." I paused. "Do you remember?"

He shook his head as if dazed. "Yeah. Bits of it. Kind of like remembering a dream. I'm not sure what's real and what's not."

"We had to do a cleansing spell on you." I nodded toward the swimming hole. "Which is why we're out here swimming in the middle of the night."

"And your parents? Did I imagine that? Are they okay?"

"Yes. We got them back. They're sleeping now. Kaylee and her dad were behind their kidnapping and the murders. They've been arrested. Everyone is safe."

"Good." He spun on his heel and walked away.

"Are you okay?" I called after him.

He paused, his back ramrod straight. "I'm fine," he growled and stalked towards his cabin.

"Will he be all right?" I asked Gran.

"He just needs a little time to re-adjust. His brain got a little scrambled," she assured me, climbing out of the swimming hole. "A good night's rest will see him right as rain. Speaking of, it's late, and this girl needs her beauty sleep."

I couldn't agree more. The adrenaline rush that had been keeping me going had well and truly worn off and exhaustion took its place. Sleep had never felt so appealing.

We were woken the following morning by someone banging on the door. Jenna scrambled out of bed, hair askew, and cautiously opened the door to find Mick standing on the other side. I sat up, wiping sleep from my eyes.

"Mick. Hi," Jenna squeaked in surprise.

"Sorry if I woke you." His eyes traveled over her, taking in the pink-and-white-checkered shorts and threadbare T-shirt she slept in.

"What time is it?" she muttered, abandoning the door to cross to the small kitchenette and put the coffee pot on. "Can't function without caffeine," she said by way of explanation.

"It's just gone nine," Mick said, still in the doorway.

"Come in, come in," I told him, throwing the covers off and sliding out of bed. "I guess you need statements and stuff?"

The door closed, and I heard his booted feet on the floor as he headed for the kitchen table. "Yes. And to check in on how you all are. Do you need medical attention?"

I shot him a look. "No. You asked last night, remember? I'm fine. Whatever she dosed me with wasn't that strong. It wore off fast." I didn't mention I'd used my magical ability to rid my body of the tranquilizer faster than a mere human could.

"Your parents seem fine too. It's remarkable."

"The Joneses are made of strong stuff," Jenna said. "Coffee?"

"Please."

I excused myself to use the bathroom. After taking care of my bladder and quickly washing my face and brushing my hair, I was semi-respectable. Jenna had coffee waiting, and I gave her a quick hug of appreciation. "Thanks, hon."

"Anytime."

We seated ourselves opposite Mick at the table and waited. He didn't disappoint. He confirmed that the containers Kaylee had placed on her makeshift altar contained the ashes of Tamir's and Beth's hearts. That Kaylee's DNA matched the other occult scenes he'd come across over the past year and that the horse tranquilizer she'd used to drug us matched the one stolen from a vet who was visiting the Arrowstrand Station a few years back.

Colin had assisted his daughter in both murders, and of course his second life in Darana was blown clean out of the water. Kaylee and Colin were being held in cells at the Arrowstrand station while detectives from Adelaide were on their way.

"They've requested that you don't leave until they've questioned you, and that you will be required to testify when the case goes to court," Mick told me.

"Hanging around for a few more days isn't a hardship," I told him. "Now I know my parents are safe, I can relax and play tourist for a while."

"Would the courts be open to a video link for her testimony?" Jenna asked.

Mick shrugged. "It's a possibility for sure. Considering all the main witnesses live in America I don't think it's an unreasonable request."

There was a light tap at the door, then it swung open to reveal Mom and Dad. "Good morning." Mom smiled. "Sergeant Gould came to visit us first, so we waited a few minutes to make sure you were up before coming over."

Jumping to my feet, I hugged them both. "You're both okay?" I asked, looking them over. They had no physical injuries that I could see and looked well rested this morning.

"We're fine, honey," Dad said, patting my shoulder. "But we could sure use a coffee. Seems someone used up the last of our coffee stash."

I knew he was teasing, but I felt a wave of guilt. "Sorry. And yes, come in, sit, I'll get you coffees."

Once we were all settled, I turned my attention back to the events of recent days. "Something that's been bugging me," I said, cupping my coffee cup between my palms. "Was Nigel involved?"

Mick shook his head. "He knew about Colin's affair. He also knew that Kaylee was responsible for the fire at the original Arrowstrand station. It's yet to be determined if charges will be laid."

We were interrupted by another knock at the door. This time it was Remy. Bandit bounced in, happy to have located Archie who was still curled up on the foot of my bed.

"I heard voices, figured you were all gathered here, and didn't want to miss out on the big reveal," Remy said, helping herself to coffee and leaning back against the kitchen cupboard, watching my parents expectantly.

"The big reveal?" Mick asked.

"The copper pyramid and the scroll," Remy said, as

if it were perfectly obvious that was what she was talking about.

Dad laughed. "Yes, we made significant progress."

"And?" Remy demanded. "Don't keep me in suspenders!"

I snorted. That was something Dad used to say.

"You always were one of my best students, Remy." Dad chuckled. "So to ease your burning curiosity, yes, we discovered the copper pyramid."

My jaw dropped. "You did? Where? We found your dig site and for the life of me I still can't fathom how a copper pyramid could be hidden down there. And the tracks from your trolley? Did they lead to a secret chamber?"

"Ah!" Mick held up a hand. "I can help with that one. The tracks were fake. Kaylee took the trolley and left the fake tracks to make it look like you had disappeared in the caves. Like Harper suggested, the tracks disappeared into a wall, leading people to believe you were trapped on the other side."

Remy's face fell. "So no secret chamber?"

Dad shook his head. "I'm afraid not."

Mom nudged him under the table. "For goodness sake, Kevin, put her out of her misery. Tell her about the pyramid."

"Yes! Tell us!" I demanded. Remy perked up again.

"I can do better than that, I can show you," Dad said, standing up.

Remy frowned. "You want to go to the caves?"

"No need." Digging in his pocket, he held out his fist and slowly uncurled his fingers. There, in his palm, was a tiny copper pyramid. I burst out laughing. *Oh, my God.* We'd been expecting a giant whopping pyramid—instead, the real thing was a miniature version of what we'd been looking for.

Remy took it from him and studied it intently.

"Do you see the engravings?" Dad asked her.

Remy nodded. "Geospirals. So you deciphered the language?"

"Enough to know that we weren't looking for your typical pyramid," Mom said.

"And what about the geospirals Kaylee used? She left a rock with a geospiral carved into it at each of the crime scenes."

Mom was shaking her head. "Kaylee got the wrong end of the stick with that. Tamir knew that the geospirals were important, but he hadn't figured out they were a language. Kaylee assumed they were part of her ritual, that everything was happening for a reason and that Tamir had appeared in her life to reveal the geospirals to her. The truth is, they have nothing to do with ancient goddesses and immortality."

"Remy, you were telling us about Dad's research, that he thought the geospirals could be linked to a portal allowing people to travel through time and space?" I asked, remembering what she'd told us in the car when we'd first arrived. "Dad, is that true?"

Dad smiled, his expression proud. "We think so. But not necessarily traveling through time, but space, yes. How much did Remy tell you?"

"That the geospirals linked two portals and when activated they formed something like a wormhole where you could travel from one side of the world to another," I answered. "That you thought the second copper scroll could be here because thousands of years ago Australia was undiscovered, no one had traveled here, so it made the perfect hiding spot."

Remy snapped her fingers. "I've got it. The copper pyramid is the key."

Dad closed his fist around the tiny pyramid and nodded. "That's what we think. It's a key in the shape of a pyramid."

"A key that will unlock what?" Jenna asked. Her phone was out, and she was making notes.

"The wormhole—for want of a better word—that will allow us to travel. Either between destinations or dimensions."

"Dimensions?" Remy breathed, eyes sparkling with anticipation.

"We think it's a possibility," Mom said. "We've got the key. The next problem is finding the lock."

Remy sagged back against the kitchen counter. "You don't think the lock is here?"

Both Mom and Dad shrugged. "We don't know. The Arrowstrand caves are definitely a portal. But is it controlled from here? We have found no indication…yet."

"Well, all of that is outside of my investigation I'm afraid," Mick said, draining his coffee and standing. "I need to get back. I just wanted to check in with you all and let you know where we're at. The Adelaide detectives will be here later today—I'm not sure if they'll want to interview you straight away or if they'll be busy with the crime scenes."

"Not a problem." Dad stood and shook Mick's hand. "Thank you for everything."

Dad saw Mick out, then paused at the door. "Didn't you want to find your mom?" he asked my mother.

"Oh yes. I thought she'd be here. Maybe she's sleeping in."

"Gran is either up at the house mothering that baby joey," I said, "or down by the swimming hole working on her tan."

Mom and Dad left to find Gran, Remy tagging along, as she wasn't done grilling them about their discovery of the copper pyramid.

"I'm going to take a shower," Jenna announced, gathering up the empty coffee cups and putting them in the sink. "Then I'm writing this up for the *Whitefall Cove Tribune.* I'm thinking I've got enough material for a series of stories."

"I'd say you've got enough for a book!" I joked. "I think I'll go check on Blake while you're using the bathroom."

"You're worried?"

I nodded. "Just a little. We didn't leave things very well last night." In fact, he'd seemed pretty angry. I wanted to clear the air with him, put things right.

"Good luck." Jenna squeezed my hand, and I watched as she gathered up some clean clothes and headed into the small bathroom at the back of the cabin. Forgetting I was still in the track pants and tank I'd slept in, I hurried two doors down to Blake's cabin and knocked.

The door sprang open, and I looked at Andi in surprise. "Oh! I was expecting Blake," I said, pressing a hand to my chest, for my heart had leaped at the sight of her.

"He checked out," Andi said, "and I need to keep busy, so I'm giving the cabin a thorough going over."

I froze for a split second. He'd checked out? Andi turned her back and went back to work. I followed her in where I could see the stripped bed, linens on the floor. The wardrobe door stood open. Empty.

"When did he check out?" I whispered, shocked that Blake had left without a word to any of us.

"Early this morning. About six." Andi paused where she was tossing the towels from the bathroom onto the growing pile of linens on the floor. "He didn't tell you?"

I shook my head. "But we've got the Land Rover. What, did he walk?"

"Nigel gave him a lift."

"To where?" Because Blake had told me when we were first planning the trip to Australia that the jet couldn't land at Arrowstrand, the airstrip wasn't big enough. Which meant he wasn't flying out. Had Nigel agreed to drive him all the way to Adelaide?

"Darana," Andi said, gathering all the linens and shoving them into a cloth sack, then pulling the drawstring tight. "I think he'd arranged a lift to the city with a truck driver from there," she added.

"Right." I didn't know what to think. Or say. Then I focused on Andi. "Are you okay? This must have been an awful shock for you... Kaylee and Colin."

Andi paused and looked at me, her eyes glassy with unshed tears. "I had no idea. No idea the two people I love most in the world were such evil, vile creatures." Crossing to the kitchen, she began a cleaning frenzy that indicated she did not want to talk about it. Swiveling on my heel, I left silently, walking back to Jenna's cabin, all the while wondering why on earth Blake would have left without saying a word.

"Oh, here she is now." Jenna was talking to someone on her laptop when I came in.

"Who's that?" I asked.

"Monica!" Jenna swiveled the laptop around so I could see the screen.

Smiling, I slid onto a chair. "Hey, Mon. It's so good to see you."

"Jenna tells me everything is sorted. You found your folks and can come home soon?"

"Yes. Happy ending for all." I smiled. "But enough about me, what about you? What's new? How's Whitefall Cove? Any exciting goss?"

Monica tapped a blood red fingernail against her chin and cast her eyes to the ceiling as if in deep thought. "Hmmmm. Let me see. Anything interesting happening in Whitefall Cove?"

I laughed. "Come on, spit it out. You're clearly dying to tell me something."

"Oh, okay!" She grinned, leaning closer to the camera. "Jackson and Liliana have split!"

"What?" Jenna and I said in unison. Jenna scrambled from her seat to scoot next to me on my chair, almost sending me tumbling to the floor. "Spill!" she demanded.

Monica laughed. "I knew that would get your attention. Okay, so here's what I know. It was Jackson who did the dumping."

"But...why?" I asked.

Monica sent me an *are you brain dead* look. "I don't know the details," she said, "but I would strongly suspect it's because he has finally come to his senses and realized he has feelings for someone else."

I sat stunned for a second. This morning had started off so well—Mom and Dad were safe, Kaylee and Colin had been arrested, then things had kinda spiraled, sending my thought processes into chaos once again. Blake had left without a word. Now Jackson had ended his relationship with Liliana. Both events threw me for a loop. Just when you thought you knew someone, it turned out you didn't.

"So what's the plan?" Monica asked.

"You know..." I hesitated, confusion vying with anticipation making me feel unsure. "I have no idea. We don't know why Jackson ended things with Liliana. If it really was him who ended things. I know how the gossip mill works and it's not always right. Or kind. Or fair."

"Yeah, but you're overlooking one thing," Jenna said.

"What's that?"

"Jackson is single."

And suddenly I had a burning desire to get my butt back to Whitefall Cove and find out exactly what had happened—and what it all meant.

"And what are you going to do about your hot, sexy, lawyer?" Monica drawled.

"Oh, that's easy. He left."

"He what?" Jenna screeched in my ear. Slapping a hand over my potentially damaged eardrum as I turned to her. "He took off early this morning."

"Without saying goodbye?" Monica asked.

I nodded. "Yup."

"Oh." Yeah. Oh. We all knew what that meant. I guess I'd never understand the mystery that was Blake Tennant. But now, new possibilities concerning one Detective Jackson Ward were suddenly, tantalizingly, within arm's reach.

"I tell you what, Harper Jones," Monica drawled. "Life is never dull with you around."

Ready to read Harper's next adventure in **Witch Way to Beauty & the Beach***? Get your copy here:*
www.JaneHinchey.com/BeautyandtheBeach

Thank you for reading! If you enjoyed this book, I'd greatly appreciate your review.

You can find a complete list of my books, including series and reading order on my website at:

www.JaneHinchey.com

Join my newsletter here:

www.JaneHinchey.com/subscribe

And finally, join my readers group on Facebook here:

www.JaneHinchey.com/LittleDevils

Thank you so much for taking a chance and reading my book . It's readers like you who make this journey worthwhile and fuel my passion for storytelling. Your support means the world to me, and I can't wait to share more exciting stories with you in the future.

xoxo

Jane

FREE BOOK OFFER

Want to get an email alert when a new book is released?

Sign up for my newsletter today,

https://janehinchey.com/subscribe

and as a bonus, receive a FREE e-book of

Cupcakes & Curses!

READ MORE BY JANE

Find them all at www.JaneHinchey.com/books

<u>The Ghost Detective Mysteries</u>

#1 Ghost Mortem

#2 Give up the Ghost

#3 The Ghost is Clear

#4 A Ghost of a Chance

#5 Here Ghost Nothing

#6 Who Ghost There?

#7 Wild Ghost Chase

#8 Easy Come, Easy Ghost

#9 Life Ghost On

<u>Witch Way Paranormal Cozy Mystery Series</u>

#1 Witch Way to Magic & Mayhem

#2 Witch Way to Romance & Ruin

#3 Witch Way Down Under

#4 Witch Way to Beauty & the Beach

#5 Witch Way to Death & Destruction

#6 Witch Way to Secrets & Sorcery

<u>**The Gravestone Mysteries**</u>

#1 Fur the Hex of it

#2 Battle of the Hexes

#3 What the Hex

<u>**The Midnight Chronicles**</u>

#1 One Minute to Midnight

#2 Two Minutes Past Midnight

#3 Third Strike of Midnight

<u>**Clean Scene Inc.**</u>

#1 All in Vein

PARANORMAL ROMANCE/URBAN FANTASY

The Awakening Trilogy

Hell's Angel Trilogy

The Enforcer Series (4 books)

Standalones

Returned

Secret Fates

Destiny's Touch

Blood Cursed

Heart of Darkness

About Jane

Hi there! I'm Jane, crafting tales of paranormal cozy mysteries sprinkled with urban fantasy romance. Between sips of coffee and dodging my mischievous cats, I immerse myself in stories where magic meets everyday life.

Once known as Zahra Stone in the world of steamy urban fantasy, I've now merged those fiery tales under the Jane Hinchey banner. Off the page you'll find me binging on true crime documentaries or sneaking in a Power Nap. Dive into my stories and join me on an enchanting journey!

Find me here: www.janehinchey.com

facebook.com/janehincheyauthor

instagram.com/janehincheyauthor

amazon.com/Jane-Hinchey/e/B0193449MI

bookbub.com/authors/jane-hinchey

goodreads.com/jane_hinchey